OH SWEDEN! OH ISRAEL!

With thanks to Malin and all my family

Oh Sweden!
Oh Israel!

Stephan Mendel-Enk

Translated from the Swedish by Michael Lundin

Portobello
BOOKS

*The author would like to thank his Swedish publisher,
Richard Herold, and the Swedish Authors' Fund.*

Published by Portobello Books 2013
Portobello Books
12 Addison Avenue
London
W11 4QR
United Kingdom

Copyright © Stephan Mendel-Enk and Bokförlaget Atlas 2010

Translation copyright © Michael Lundin 2013

First published in Swedish under the title *Tre Apor* in 2010 by
Bokförlaget Atlas, Stockholm, Sweden

The rights of Stephan Mendel-Enk to be identified as the author of
this work and of Michael Lundin to be identified as the translator
of this work have been asserted by them in accordance with the
Copyright, Designs and Patents Act 1988.

A CIP catalogue record for this book is available from the British Library.

1 3 5 7 9 10 8 6 4 2

ISBN 978 1 84627 415 2

Typeset by Avon DataSet Limited, Bidford on Avon, Warwickshire
Printed and bound by CPI Group (UK) Ltd, Croydon, CR0 4YY

Grandma had been lying in cold storage at the mortuary for two days and no one had thought to ask the rabbi to bless the place.

The traffic lights outside Sahlgrenska Hospital had just turned green when Aunt Laura mentioned it. Mum wound down the window and lit a thin white cigarette with her gold-plated lighter. She wasn't about to take the blame. She had notified the relatives, she had made arrangements for the food afterwards. However, she said, there was one person in the car who was without employment during the day. Maybe *she* could have rung the rabbi if she'd suddenly become so pious.

Aunt Laura leaned over Mirra and me and thumped Mum on the thigh. Grandpa told them to calm down, while Rafael accelerated up the hill towards Guldheden, down through the city, past the No. 3 tram's final stop and into the narrow passageway that led to the gravel car park.

A gentle breeze blew over the headstones in Gothenburg's Jewish cemetery. Thin raindrops were carried with it on the air.

Moshe Dayan leaned his broom against the chapel wall. He used his one eye to give us a knowing funereal wink. He was over eighty years old, with white hair, a bent back and long, claw-like fingers. The pirate's eyepatch was all he had in common with the real Moshe Dayan.

We were allowed ten minutes to ourselves in there, he said. No photos, no cigarettes, *fershteyn*?

The rusty handle was pressed down and the chapel's two dark-brown doors opened wide. Everything looked smaller, but apart from that it was exactly as I remembered. The smell of damp wood, the large Star of David on the far wall, the yellow glow behind it.

1

The last time it had been jam-packed, with people in large groups by the walls and the air so heavy that the windows had steamed up. Now the chapel was empty. In front of the Star of David lay Grandma in an open coffin. Her dry skin was pulled tight over her cheekbones. Mum and Aunt Laura sat with foreheads touching on either side at the top end of the coffin. They held each other by the shoulders and watered Grandma's thin skin with their tears. They each grabbed hold of one of her lifeless arms, praising her well-manicured fingernails. They squeezed the hands which had stroked the ground in Trelleborg's harbour and copied out recipes from the weekly edition of *Hemmets veckotidning*.

'I want to kiss her. Can you kiss her? Rafael, what does the Talmud say?'

Laura's head was only a few inches above her mother's face. When she didn't receive the go-ahead, she decided that it was allowed anyway. She put her hands around Grandma's face and covered her cheeks with lipstick marks that she then caressed away with her thumb.

She pulled out a grey miniature camera from her inside pocket. She pressed the button a few times to no avail. She climbed up on her chair, but the camera still didn't work, and shaking it didn't help either. She dried the lens on the arm of her jacket and said she should have brought her Polaroid instead.

Mum rummaged in her handbag for her own camera and said that the correct pronunciation was Paul – air – royd.

'Pola – row – eed, little Debbele.'

'Paul – air – royd,' said Mum. It was an American brand. It should be pronounced the American way.

Aunt Laura informed Mum that she'd lived in New York for thirty years and if it really was pronounced in that *meshugenah* way she would probably have picked it up by now. Without lifting her eyes from her handbag, Mum said that she probably would have, had she met regularly with other people. Like at a workplace, for instance.

My watch said it was slightly past quarter to eleven. The ten minutes Moshe Dayan had promised us were up.

Aunt Laura squatted on the chair and asked my siblings and me to stand behind the coffin. 'Your mother's very clever,' she said, and pushed the camera button. 'Imagine being so good at English just by living in Gothenburg.' She mimicked Mum's Swedish-English accent and couldn't stop herself from laughing.

Mum's nostrils and eyes widened. Her chin shot forward. She waved a fist at Laura, who quickly pulled back, stumbled and flung out a hand towards the back of her chair. For a second it looked as if she would regain her balance. The next moment she fell face first into the coffin.

Everything was in place when the ceremony started barely half an hour later. Grandma's sisters were there with their families. Old uncles in flat caps sat with their legs splayed wide and walking sticks in front of them. Aunties with sweet perfumes handed out paper tissues. By the rear wall, at a comfortable distance from Mum, sat people I hadn't met for over a decade.

After the prayers, the rabbi praised Grandma for her pastries, which had often brightened the congregation's Saturday *kiddush*, as well as for her contribution to card-playing. Used tissues fell to the floor; packets of fresh ones were passed around.

I was one of the six men who carried the coffin through the cemetery. We walked up the hill and stopped next to a large hole in the ground located slightly above the car park. When it was my time to throw earth on to the coffin I tried to think of Grandma, but everything was overshadowed by the last time I'd gone through this ritual. The long procession of people who had trailed behind me when I'd lifted the shovel that time. The winter haze that burdened the sky; the embraces of the grown-ups. Just come by. Any time you like. Bring your sister.

3

I handed over the shovel. The wind blew through the naked branches that separated our cemetery from the churchyard next door.

Bulka with poppy seeds was used to mop up the leftovers from the plates. We had run out of salmon quite quickly and also of egg salad, as well as most of the chopped liver which Aunt Betty had brought.

A shiny tablecloth covered the table. The dark-silver candlesticks stood in the middle.

The salt and pepper pots were new. They remained unused for the duration of the meal, located next to Papa Moysowich's wine glass. In front of Rafael, the prayer book lay open. He had rolled up his shirt sleeves and placed one arm on the back of the chair next to him. In his hand he held a slice of *bulka* from which he occasionally pulled off pieces he then pushed into his mouth.

Mum was dressed in a black, slightly glittery outfit. She wore large bangles which rattled when she reached across the table.

Ingemar wore a diagonally striped tie that matched his dark-blue trousers. Occasionally he would get up and walk around the table to make sure that everything was all right. Each time he passed my seat, he adjusted the rug under the table with his foot.

A faction in the corner had sneaked a head start on Mama Moysowich's coconut cookies, which were waiting on top of the blue drinks cabinet. Aunt Laura opened the cabinet and pulled out a number of bottles, together with my scratched *kiddush* cup which she found in there. She asked what had happened to it, but failed to get an answer.

Pink napkins were pulled out of the napkin holder, then scrunched up and dropped on to crossed cutlery. A tray with milk, sugar and shallow cups was carried in from the kitchen.

Grandpa was taking his afternoon nap in the large bedroom on the floor above. Mirra had the room next door. The door was open. Smooth apricot-coloured pillows were stacked under the floral bedcover. The desk by the window contained diaries of hers that still lay in the bottom drawer.

I lifted out some and set them down on the floor. Almost every volume looked the same. Blonde girls in straw hats on the cover, large round letters on the inside, margins filled with curly-haired princesses.

I found the sky-blue one in the middle of the pile. I knew long sections of it by heart. The text was full of childish observations that had gained a new meaning after what had happened: 'At Jacob's rehearsal Mum and Dad held each other's hands'; 'Today Mum's boss had dinner with us'; 'Dad said we might go and visit Rafael after Hanukkah. Maybe we'll be away for the whole of the Christmas holidays!'

Despite the years that had gone by, Mum still spoke in words of one syllable when the past was brought up. She still crossed the street if she saw one of her old friends from the congregation. And at the Jewish elderly care home sat Mame, confused and sedated beyond all understanding.

I remained on the floor, surrounded by the diaries, until I heard a shout from below.

I had my bar mitzvah two weeks after my thirteenth birthday. It was at the beginning of August. The garden smelled strongly of roses and we drove to the synagogue with the windows down.

We lived in a bright yellow terraced house about six miles from the city. Two floors with brown furniture, soft sofas, Italian gramophone records, Mum's chicken soup divided into portions and stored in the freezer, books, photo albums, mail order catalogues and comics on the book shelves, *mezuzot* by the doors, paintings of bearded violin players and yellow lamps that stuck out from the frames.

Mum and Dad had bought the house a few months before Mirra was born. Rafael was given a room of his own, while I had to share the one next door with a cot that would soon belong to my new sibling. I remember that Dad's toolbox was often lying about when we first moved into the house, and a snowball fight that we had in the garden after the first snowfall. One night when I awoke and quickly crossed the tiny hall in order to snuggle up between Mum and Dad, I discovered that their bed was empty. I called for them, until I heard Rafael shout that I should come in and lie next to him instead. Early in the morning we were woken up by Dad, who leaned over us, wearing his overcoat. He told us that we had a little sister.

Soon after we moved in, the whole area was filled with Jews. The Grien family bought a house on the other side of the small copse; Kreutz and Moysowich moved into the block above the play area; our closest friends, Bernie and Teresza Friedkin, purchased a low brick house less than a quarter of an hour's walk from us.

Mum had a part-time job at an office close to Gothenburg's

main street, Avenyn. In the evenings she studied at an adult education centre. She had quit secondary school and hitchhiked to Rome at the age of seventeen. After a few months she had got a job as a waitress and met Gigi, a long-haired actor who rode a motorbike. After a few months more she was pregnant. They got married at the town hall in Piazza Nuova, with all Gigi's theatre company as witnesses.

Grandma wanted Mum to write to her every week after Rafael was born. Mum wrote about his first smile, his first tooth, that he only occasionally woke up and screamed at night. She wrote that he could sit quietly for hours and play with a wallet, or a bunch of keys, while she did the ironing and folded the clothes. She didn't mention how mundane her life had become. That her days didn't comprise much beyond making breakfast, doing the washing, doing the shopping, making lunch and pushing the rickety pram along desolate streets in order to leave Gigi in peace and quiet for his siesta. Or that she sometimes found traces of mascara on the sheets when she made their bed in the afternoons.

Grandma and Grandpa came to visit a few days before Rafael's third birthday. They ate dinner at a restaurant in the neighbourhood. When Grandpa had finished eating, Grandma told him to take Rafael to the fountain in the square in front of the restaurant. She sat next to Mum, so that they were both facing the square and the children who were chasing pigeons over the old cobblestones. Grandpa and Rafael bought a little brown paper bag of seeds to feed the birds. Grandma asked Mum how she was feeling. She didn't believe her answer and asked Mum to remove her sunglasses.

Gigi was working and so wasn't at home when they got to the flat. Grandma and Grandpa helped Mum to carry her bags down to the street.

Back in Gothenburg, Mum and Rafael moved into Grandma

and Grandpa's flat at Odinsplatsen. After about a year, a one-bedroom flat became vacant in the building the congregation owned on Tredje Långgatan.

Dad was studying medicine at the time. One day, on his way home from the hospital, he saw Mum walk past on the street through the window of a tram. He recognized her from the congregation; she had been a few classes above him for Hebrew lessons but they had never talked to each other. He jumped off the tram. When he caught up with her he asked if she wanted to help at a Jewish youth festival he and his friends were arranging.

They became a couple on the last day of the festival. A large photo showing them sitting with their arms around each other, sunburned and smiling, surrounded by other festival-goers, was pinned up above the washing machine in our house. It shared one of its pins with a set of photo-booth pictures in which Rafael, Mirra and I are all sticking our tongues out.

Mum and Dad continued to involve themselves in congregation activities. In the evenings our living room was often filled with friends slouching on the sofa. They planned family camps, football tournaments, large *shabbat* dinners. Sometimes they were joined by a dissident Russian or an American visiting lecturer in a corduroy jacket who would be invited to stay the night.

My door was always a few inches ajar. I would lie with my face towards the crack of light, listening to the voices from downstairs: English, Swedish, occasional words in Yiddish and Hebrew which rose with the cigarette smoke up the stairs and mixed with the sound of the TV and Mirra's deep breaths.

At least once a week, when Dad worked nights and Mum had evening classes, Grandma and Grandpa took care of us. They came in a car loaded with indigestion tablets, sweeteners, magazines, indoor shoes, plastic bowls and chocolate bars. After dinner they made tea in the coffee percolator and watched TV.

Sometimes Mame and Grandad came instead. On other occasions they were all there together, applauding Mirra and me, who had dressed up, performing in front of them in the living room.

In the summer, after he had taken his exams, Rafael emigrated to Israel. We read his airmail letters around the kitchen table, and put a picture of him in his soldier's uniform on the fridge. I wrote to him on his own old Snoopy writing paper, told him how IFK Gothenburg Football Club were doing, then summarized the music charts.

In her second year at junior school, Mirra started to dance. In her third year, she was chosen to be part of the small children's group which was allowed to practise at Storan Concert Hall. Mum had finished her studying and, after a few short-lived jobs, she was chosen from among hundreds of applicants to be the manager's assistant at the West Sweden Chamber of Commerce. Dad regularly had articles published in academic journals while he was working on a doctoral degree in Internal Medicine. He was awarded his PhD at a very grand ceremony at City Hall.

The afternoon his colleague phoned, I was sitting at the desk in my room. I was home on my own, trying to put a roll of film in the camera I'd been given for my bar mitzvah. After a couple of rings, I got up and ran the ten or so steps to the hall. The phone was on a high wooden table that had been painted white next to a green sofa studded with corduroy buttons. I lifted the receiver at the same time as I sat down on the arm of the sofa. The voice on the other end asked if Mum was there. Then he introduced himself.

It was only when the man gave me his number for the second time that I picked up one of the pens that lay next to the phone. I then took the phone book from the lowest of the three shelves beneath the table. Almost the whole cover was filled with scribbled numbers and cartoon doodles of men. I wrote the six numbers in the top right-hand corner. When the call was over, I tore off the corner of the phone book, walked downstairs and put the piece of paper on the bench in the kitchen, in front of the radio.

I got up from the floor and ran downstairs. It was Mirra who had shouted. She was standing at the living-room window and tapping her index finger against the glass. 'Grandad's car,' she kept repeating. On the street outside. She'd seen it drive past.

I stood next to her. I was sure she was mistaken, and so was everyone else. Sighs and humourless laughter spread through the room, showing just how unconvincing her testimony was considered. However, after about thirty seconds, Grandad appeared behind the hedge at the front, leaning on Aunt Irene as he made his way to the house.

Aunt Irene helped him to struggle out of his coat. His lips were pursed and his body language was reminiscent of Yitzhak Rabin's when he was forced to shake hands with Arafat outside the White House. He called Mirra and me to his side, gave us each a fierce cuddle, took a deep breath and limped into the living room.

He stood in the middle of the room, polished his black horn-rimmed glasses with his shirt, then said that he wasn't going to start until everyone was present. This clearly referred to Mum, but the fact that he found himself in her home didn't seem to affect his decision never to utter her name again. He stood for a long time on the same spot, swaying slightly on his lopsided hip.

Mum came downstairs from the toilet, having applied a fresh layer of lipstick. A smile which didn't look in the least strained, though it must have been, lit up her face. Grandad stared at the floor while Mum sat down in the armchair. Ingemar stood behind her with a firm grip on the back of the chair.

'*Nu?*' said Grandad in a low voice.

He took a folded piece of paper from the inside pocket of his jacket, then started slowly to open it. He cleared his throat and began to read.

Bernie Friedkin's shop was long and narrow, with deep shelves along all the walls and miniature rotating displays on the floor. At the back, behind the till, was a small room with an individual hotplate, as well as a fridge. There was a bowl of sweets on the table, close to a large pastel-coloured ashtray that was decorated with the logos of different clothing brands. Bernie held the *kiddush* cup by its stem, then squinted at it from below at an angle, spinning it round in his hand.

Bernie was Dad's oldest friend. They had grown up just a few blocks from each other and had shared a flat when Dad was studying to become a doctor. During those years, Bernie had worked part-time at a company that restored furniture. Ever since then, the congregation's members came to him whenever they had something that needed to be repaired. He used to walk around the small room behind the till, mimicking their shambling gait and broken Swedish: 'Bernie, help me with Granny's candlesticks', 'Bernie, take a look at Granny's Seder dish.' As if he didn't have anything else to do. As if the clothes shop was just an excuse to allow him to mess about with their antiques. Sometimes he would climb up on a chair, pull out a cardboard box from the top shelf, then bang it down on the table so that the dust swirled up around it in thin clouds. The cardboard box was full of old *menorahs*, *hanukkiahs* with missing arms, necklaces that couldn't be fastened. Bernie used to point to the end of the box, where the word 'congregation' was written in green felt-tip pen, and say that one day he'd cross it out and write 'rubbish' instead.

The *kiddush* cup glittered under the lamp. Bernie frowned, his forehead creased into tiny wrinkles. He had already put on his glasses, then taken out a yellow tube and a little black brush from a transparent plastic case. Holding the brush between his thumb and index finger, he worked viscous fluid into the scratch which ran along one side of the cup.

Dad watched with his elbows on the table, holding his hands knotted beneath his chin. People often said we resembled one another. Sometimes I could see it myself. We had the same brown-green eyes, along with eyebrows which tightened when we concentrated. His face was a bit longer than mine, but I had inherited his broad nose and that irritating thick, curly hair which was impossible to shape into any of the hairstyles I wanted.

When the coffee percolator behind his back had stopped bubbling, Bernie poured out a cup for himself and Dad, before taking a carton of juice from the refrigerator. I stopped him quickly. I wanted coffee too, and was careful to convey this in a tone that said there was nothing at all remarkable about the fact. Bernie looked at Dad for a long time before he poured me a cup.

I pulled out an old newspaper from the pile under the table and turned to the sports pages.

Bernie and Dad talked in hushed tones. About flats that could be rented, the cost of those you could buy and when Dad would begin working again. There were only a few weeks left until the main holidays. Dad apologized because he couldn't reach a firm decision about which of the evenings we would celebrate together with Bernie's family. He explained that he would need to talk with Mum about it. Bernie said that Teresza had called again, but that Mum had slammed the phone down on her. They spoke so quietly that they were almost whispering. Ingemar's name came up. I felt the way Dad shifted his gaze towards me.

Bernie's teaspoon scraped against the bottom of the cup. After having been quiet for a while, he began to talk about a

15

woman who'd come to the shop. I recognized her name; it was some old acquaintance or nurse with whom Dad had worked, and I had to make an effort to look as if the newspaper was absorbing all of my attention. I carefully went through every single match on the results page. England, Division 1. Sweden, Division 2. Bundesliga. Werder Bremen 5–0 Vfb Stuttgart. FC Cologne 0–0 Leverkusen. Nuremberg 1–1 Waldhof Mannheim.

'What's up with her?' said Dad.

1–0 (Andersen, 27). 1–1 (Neun, 28). Attendance: 22,000.

'I said she could call.'

Dad didn't say anything. When I peeked up, I saw Bernie sitting with his middle finger sideways under his mouth, while he rested his index finger against the side of his nose. His head was angled towards the shop door. Strong light was shining in through the diamond-shaped pane and you could hear the shop assistant putting out clothes. Metal hangers clinked against each other on the low clothes rail.

When Bernie noticed that I was looking at him, he shook his head as if I'd wakened him from a deep sleep. Then he knocked on the table. 'What shall we do with your dad?' he asked me. It had been the same story ever since they were little. Other boys had to fight to get the girls to notice they even existed, but he – Bernie pointed at Dad – just batted his eyelashes and they came swarming like the locusts in Egypt. Jewish girls, *shikses*, all kinds, and he was always just as fussy. 'Sometimes I wonder if he isn't a little bit…' Bernie wobbled his left hand from side to side. 'You know.' One of his eyes narrowed; a lopsided grin appeared at the corner of his mouth. 'A *feygele*. Maybe boys suit him better. Maybe it's one of those we should get him.'

Dad raised his coffee cup, smiled and pretended that it was an alternative he was seriously considering.

At Mame and Grandad's dinner was served at seven o'clock. At half-past seven you turned on the news to see if there was anything about Israel.

Grandad watched with furrowed brow, ready to clasp his hands in case the news was bad. Which he and the other grown-ups were always convinced it would be.

They had explained it was a turbulent time. A dangerous time. Uncertain. I couldn't remember when they'd ever said it was anything else. It was always extremely uncertain, extremely charged, extremely precarious; the situation in the Knesset was always extremely unstable, and it was always being led by an extremely incompetent prime minister. Yitzhak Shamir was a hysterical dwarf. Shimon Peres couldn't even gain the respect of a Scandinavian left-wing volunteer with his *nebbishdikke* hangdog eyes.

Next to the sofa in the living room was a piano. The opposite wall was covered by a brown bookcase. There were hundreds of books on the shelves. Colour photo books from when Israel celebrated its twentieth, twenty-fifth, thirtieth and thirty-fifth anniversaries. One shelf with titles such as *The Arab-Israeli Conflict* and *The Arab-Israeli Wars*. Books on Israeli art and Israeli cookery. Thin brochures about Israel's flora and fauna, interspersed between novels about the early Zionists, Ben-Gurion's *My Life*, Golda Meir's *My Life*, Moshe Dayan's *The Story of My Life*, as well as an anniversary publication from Israeli State Television: *15 Years of High-Quality Entertainment*.

Mame walked back and forth behind Grandad's chair, muttering her ominous predictions. It would soon be over. She was certain. She could read between the lines and see the signs in the newspaper. Israel would be wiped out. At any moment now hostile neighbours would carry out their threats and raze Israel to the ground. Soon afterwards the Nazis would wake from their sleep and, like a maddened swarm of wasps, stream once more across Europe. Via the autobahn, then across the Baltic, they would roar past the hills in Slottsskogen Park, tear round by the corner shop, smash the door of the building, break into the flat, overturn the bookcase, rip down the carefully cut-out newspaper articles by the pro-Israeli politician Per Ahlmark that were stuck on the fridge, empty the blue and white collecting box on the window ledge and bring to a bloody end our latest break for freedom.

The flat consisted of four rooms. Grandad and Mame slept in a long, narrow bedroom with a blue mat, along with black and white photographs on top of a circular chest of drawers. In one of the pictures, Dad was three and Aunt Irene was six. She had curly hair and no front teeth. Dad sat on a table next to her, wearing a bow tie, with his hair flattened. On the other side of the living room was the room Dad shared with Aunt Irene when he was little and into which he had now returned. In this room was the desk where Grandad wrote his letters to the congregation's newsletter, as well as the only phone in the flat. When the news had finished, Dad went into the room to make some calls and Mame went into the kitchen to do the dishes.

They had cable TV, so I switched channels back and forth between MTV and Eurosport. The remote was massive and completely wrapped in plastic. Grandad looked at me with a worried expression on his face while I struggled to push down the correct button through the plastic. He leaned forward slightly as though about to say something. But his hip protested and he sank back down into his chair.

It was his job that had ruined his hip. For thirty years he'd sat in his car, five or six days a week, and driven all around

Scandinavia with his buttons on the back seat. Business was booming for a while in the 1950s; then came the *farkakte* zip, which destroyed everything. The zip was the biggest con the housewives of the Western world had ever been exposed to, according to Grandad. If one of those small metal tags broke you had to throw a whole pair of trousers away. Compare that with a button. A button could fall off and be sewn back on as many times as you liked. Buttons came in lots of variations: two-hole, four-hole, metal, wooden, stone, triangular, rectangular, or elongated like the toggle on a duffel coat.

All of the furniture in the flat had been bought during the heyday of the button. None of it had ever been changed and things weren't moved lightly. They had a balcony which nobody ever went out on and a record player that was never used. They had been given an LP by Mum and Dad as a Hanukkah present once. They had placed it behind the record player as though it were a painting. I used to get Mirra to ask Mame if we could listen to it. Just as much as I wanted to hear the music, I wanted to see the stereo lights come on and the turntable spin on their bookshelf. 'Ask her when the right moment comes,' I said to Mirra the first time she returned with Mame's answer. The next time I said, 'Say that we'll take it back if she isn't going to listen to it.' That was the last time I tried, because Mame got so angry that she came out of the kitchen, snatched the record from my hands and pushed it back behind the record player.

Both she and Grandad spoke Yiddish when they got angry. I didn't like Yiddish. There was something embarrassing built in to the language. The word for fart was *forts*, for instance. I didn't understand the point of having a word which sounded as unpleasant as the phenomenon it described. *Forts*. Every time you pronounced it, it was as if you had performed the action all over again.

Grandad snatched the remote control from my hand. The rapid movement made him grunt and he had to sit quietly for a while to recover after he'd pressed the off button and the screen had gone blank.

He turned to face me. My hands were squeezed flat by the large cushions of flesh which comprised his palms. When I was younger he used to grip my upper arms hard and lift me up on to his knee. He had large, soft lips which he let loose on my face, covering it in kisses. Afterwards you smelled of dishcloth. Grandad refused to restrict his lips in any way. The fact that I continually struggled to escape his grip didn't bother him. He didn't see mutual attraction as a necessary prerequisite for the physical expression of love.

Sometimes he had urgent stories to tell. They usually began chronologically and comprehensibly, but he would soon lose himself in digressions about people he'd known a long time ago, or in anecdotes about unresolved conflicts with avaricious wholesalers the endings of which he'd forgotten. Mame would shake her head and say, 'It wasn't like that at all. Stop lying to the boy,' and he would hiss, 'What do you know? This was long before I met you,' and then they would start speaking Yiddish.

Now Grandad wanted to hear the latest development in the relationship that had been discovered between Mum and her boss. Above all, he wanted to know if they had mentioned anything about getting a Christmas tree. Christmas was still several months away, but Grandad was worried, because he knew how quickly you could be transformed into someone from Västerås if you weren't careful.

People from Västerås had come to my bar mitzvah. It was at those kinds of events that they appeared. Fiftieth birthdays, weddings and funerals. Every family had a few: distant relations who had become completely assimilated, living in some strange place in the Swedish countryside. They had dry handshakes, names like Björn and Ulrika, and were either teetotallers or raging alcoholics.

A Christmas tree might seem harmless, but it could be the

first domino in a row which, when it fell, would drag you down with it, down the precipice of loneliness and into the valley of emptiness, past the frozen silence and the darkness of restlessness, until one morning you awoke with haggard eyes and Västerås city centre outside your window.

Grandad's serious expression, together with the doom-laden tone in his voice, worried me too, but I wasn't about to admit it. 'He can have a Christmas tree if he wants,' was all I said. Grandad looked at me without replying. After a while, he recalled a story about a Jewish man whose son wanted to become a Christian. Grandad really wanted to tell me the story, but he got confused by the beginning, and he couldn't remember if it was the son who talked with the father or the father who talked with God; then he put his hand to his head, before asking me to wait.

Mame opened the door to the kitchen a fraction and said I could come in and help her dry the dishes.

She scrubbed a plate with the washing-up brush. The same plate again and again. Curses poured out from the corner of her mouth.

Her fingers were small and as stubby as gherkins. Her nails were painted a fierce deep red, ending quite a bit below the tips of her fingers. She'd had a disease which made her hands shake. They shook so much that she couldn't play the piano any more. It was a tragedy, she felt. Without music she was only half a person.

But the shaking didn't stop her from drawing. In the mornings she sat at the kitchen table and drew apples, the view of the courtyard or something from her imagination. I never told her that I used to draw too. I didn't want to be like Mame. She was a bit crazy. Her table manners were a disaster. She made deep squelching sounds when she ate. She also liked to talk with her food halfway down her gullet. It was hard to know whether she was in the middle of swallowing or vomiting. When she removed chicken bones from her mouth, she held her head low over her plate and spat. She didn't stop talking then either. Always about dreadful things, serious things, principles that she definitely wasn't about to abandon and people she'd definitely seen through.

The colour of her face got darker as she talked. She'd always known that Mum was the wrong woman for Dad, she said. She had told him not to marry her, but he hadn't listened. No one did. They thought they could treat her any way they liked. Grandma, whom she'd trusted. Grandpa, of whom she'd held such a high opinion. They had both let her down. They should have talked sense into their daughter, she said to me. Not fire up her *mishegas*.

Mame dropped the brush into the water so heavily that suds foamed up over the worktop. She grabbed my T-shirt, then said that she'd never be able to look either Grandma or my mother in the eyes again. She was staring at me while the words hissed out of her mouth. I wanted to look away, but didn't dare. 'He should have listened to me. I knew how it would end from the beginning. Do you hear me, Coybele? Right from the beginning!'

'As Chairman,' Grandad began, before immediately being forced to start again, because Betty said she hadn't heard.

'As Chairman of the Disciplinary Board of Chevra Kadisha, the burial society of the Jewish Congregation of Gothenburg, it is my role to inform members of the congregation which rules apply regarding visits to the grounds and properties the congregation owns at Östra Kyrkogården 12:3, hereafter referred to as the Jewish cemetery.'

He lowered his hand, which was still holding the piece of paper. Fixing his gaze somewhere above his audience, he said that our situation was remarkable. We found ourselves in a new millennium, we communicated via computers and cordless phones, but the problems we faced as a *chevra* in the diaspora were the same today as they had been for 2,000 years. In other words:

anti-Semitic vandalism;
late payments;
lack of space.

The final point was starting to become ever more alarming, he went on, once again looking at his piece of paper. The graves were already packed together as tightly as possible. The number of elderly members in the congregation was high, yet the unstable situation in the Middle East meant that insufficient people – from the *chevra*'s perspective – were emigrating to Israel.

Opposing the congregation's wish for more land was the church next door, which feared that anti-Semitic graffiti would spill over on to their graves by mistake. Besides, the church was also unhappy about the inappropriate noises that emanated from the car park next to the Jewish cemetery; noises that, they assumed, would increase with any expansion.

Grandad raised his voice. The council had let it be understood that an expansion would:

1. be very expensive, and
2. necessitate more disciplined behaviour from all of us with regard to funerals.

Together, these points forced the burial society to take stern action against various things. These included late payments, as well as indiscreet behaviour in and around the cemetery.

'In other words, it also includes,' said Grandad, before pausing slightly, 'incidents of the sort which occurred in the chapel today.'

I used to get off at Drottningtorget Square and take the route along the canal. Other stops were closer, but I liked walking there, by myself, picking up small pebbles and throwing them into the water. Couples sat on blankets between the crooked trees on the other side. Gangs of punks with ghetto-blasters and cans of beer ventured all the way down to the canal's edge.

On the street opposite, there was a porn shop with covered-up windows. The door was always wide open and a large Swedish flag hung cheerfully over the entrance. Next door was a record store which smelled of damp clothes.

I usually bought a Snickers bar, or a Twix, along with some chewing gum from the lady in the kiosk. She had brown glasses with a faint line across the lenses. She thought we were so well brought up. She was never worried when we appeared. With other kids she couldn't relax a second. She'd bend down to get a packet of crisps and by the time she stood up again the bowl with lollipops would be empty. We never did that. It was in our genes, she believed.

Opposite the congregation building's entrance there was a multi-storey car park with a barrier, striped like a barber's pole, that was slowly raised and then lowered. A foggy cloud of exhaust fumes was expelled from the car park. Just in front of the congregation's doorway they merged with the sticky-sweet smell of food from the Chinese restaurants at both ends of the street. It smelled at its very best immediately after it had stopped raining.

Zelda had her basket in the passageway just inside the security barrier. She jumped up when I came in, wagging her tail, with her thick tongue hanging from her mouth. The exercise made her so hungry that she then lumbered straight in past the broad, white venetian blinds that hung in front of Zaddinsky's office, before begging for sugar-free digestive biscuits from the packet on his desk. I heard them gently quarrelling in there. Zaddinsky tried to sound stern, but couldn't hide his gratitude at being given a break from work. When I passed by, he stuck his round head through the blinds to comment on my clothes, my haircut or my large rucksack: 'Tee, hee… is it you who's carrying the bag, or is the bag carrying you?'

The classroom was on the third floor. It was the second door on the left down a corridor with green and yellow walls. Work completed by previous students had been put up all around the room. There were badly copied photos. Lined pages with facts jotted down in careful handwriting. Ben-Gurion lost his mother at eleven years of age… Moshe Dayan lost his eye during the Second World War… Despite her disguise, Golda Meir was not able to reach the Jordanian prince with her message…

In total there were twelve of us who, from this autumn, would meet every week on a Thursday evening for two hours' study about Israel. We would met at the same time, on the same day, and were the same group of twelve pupils who had been coming together for the previous seven years to study Hebrew and the Jewish religion.

Just as before, Miss Judith was our teacher. She had long dark hair which was held back with a large clip at her neck. For the most part she wore tight trousers made of a shiny material. She had pulled them up high over her midriff, so it looked as if she had two stomachs: one above and one below her thin belt. While she waited for the cigarettes she would smoke in the break, she kept her hands occupied with a pen or a piece of chalk.

During the coming year she would teach us all about modern Israel – its history, geography, political system and most important exports – and also help us to collect the money that was needed to go on a five-week-long trip to Israel in the summer.

My seat was the second-furthest back, in the row closest to the door. I sat next to Jonathan Friedkin. We'd also been in the same class at junior school and the first years of secondary school. I used to walk home with him in the afternoons a few days a week. Under his bed, he had a whole box full of American comics and music magazines, which he'd been given by a relative. One warm afternoon in spring, we were playing football with his younger brother in the garden when Teresza, his mother, came home. She collected the post from the mailbox, then looked through the letters on her way to the door. She stopped on the little stone steps in front of the entrance and read aloud from one of the letters that Jonathan had been accepted by a school in the city.

Jonathan continued to play without saying anything. Teresza walked up to us and repeated the news. To begin with, her voice sounded more enthusiastic, then questioning, before getting annoyed. After a while, she too became quiet. She told us to follow her inside. She picked out a small blue and white pamphlet from a pile of paper on the worktop. It was from a Jewish youth group and Teresza showed us all the camps and parties in which we could participate now we'd become teenagers.

We'd spent the previous summer at a four-week-long Jewish summer camp in Denmark. At Christmas we might be going to a camp in Skåne. For half-term we'd see if the congregation in Stockholm was arranging a skiing trip.

Despite all this, Jonathan hadn't yet decided if he was going to move to Israel with me after we'd finished our exams. I was going to go immediately, only a month or so after finishing secondary school, just as Rafael had done. Grandad had praised this decision in his speech at my bar mitzvah. 'I cannot emphasize strongly enough the joy it gives us that you have already expressed such a clear desire to have a Jewish future.' His speech was a long one and I'd had difficulty concentrating on it. Dad had nodded approvingly when the waiter paused at my seat with his bottle of wine, and I had raised my glass for a 'L'chaim' every time I made eye contact with someone in the room.

When I awoke that morning, on the day of the bar mitzvah, I'd been in a joyous mood. When I went up in the synagogue to give my reading, the rabbi asked if I was nervous. I didn't understand what he meant. What on earth could I be nervous about? We had practised for half a year. I knew my portion of the Torah as if it were tattooed across my soul. The rabbi had laughed when he realized I didn't understand his question.

Mum and I had bought the clothes I was wearing. A short-sleeved shirt, pale trousers and a red tie. My shoes had a checked pattern, with two tassels on top. They'd cost a bit more but, as Mum had remarked, I could use them for school afterwards. They would go well with my jeans.

Almost all the bar and bat mitzvah parties I'd ever been to had a moment, part-way through the dinner, when someone in the family stood up and said something spontaneous. Something that wasn't quite a traditional speech but rather an impulse they'd had while eating, which they felt an immediate need to share. Speeches like that started off just like the normal ones: they praised the bar mitzvah boy for his excellent achievement on the day, then expressed their gratitude for being at the party, as well as being able to partake of the delicious food. When that bit was over, they usually clasped their hands under their chin, looked down at the table and said: But…

At the point they uttered that word they became hoarse and they were forced to pause and catch their breath for a moment. When they were able to speak again, they mentioned the name of some deceased old relative. After that happened, the floodgates opened. The rest of what they had to say came out through uncontrollable tears. It was so sad that the dead person wasn't there to share this moment. The dead person would really have appreciated it. The dead person had had such a special and close link to the person at the centre of the day's proceedings.

No one said anything like that at my bar mitzvah. Everybody was there – Grandma and Grandpa, Grandad and Mame, Aunt Irene and Aunt Laura, Mum and Dad, Rafael and Mirra – sitting side by side at the head table at the far end of the room. Dad nudged my elbow, which kept wanting to slide over the arm of my chair. Mum patted my cheek. Grandad leaned past her when he'd finished speaking. He gave me his speech and said I could read it when I got back home.

During my first year in Israel I planned to work on a kibbutz. I was going to learn Hebrew properly. I intended to take care of the animals or help in the kitchen. I imagined that there would be a piece of paper on a sun-bleached noticeboard outside the dining room. I would sign up my name and one evening I'd be called to a meeting on a lawn, to listen to a scarred colonel who'd seen and done it all. He'd tell us that he didn't want to lie to us. He didn't want to pretend that it was just heroism and glory which awaited us; there were other things too. There was a terrible side, a dangerous side. He'd tell us to make sure that we knew what we were doing, what we were letting ourselves in for. He'd approach each of us individually for private chats, stopping in front of me, squatting on the soft evening grass. I'd look towards the barracks that were a bit off in the distance, where my friends and I used to spend most evenings; where we smoked, talked and sang in flickering candlelight, with the throbbing of the crickets around us and the endless Israeli night sky stretching above. I would tell the colonel that I understood the time for games was over. That serious matters awaited me: it was my fate, one cannot run from what it is one has to do. '*Mazel tov*,' the colonel would say, then put his arm around me. 'Welcome on board.'

I longed for that day. Most of all, I longed to return home

for the summer. I would come walking down the corridor, having gone through passport control at the airport, towards the escalator that leads to baggage reclaim, wearing a green shirt with yellow Hebrew letters on my chest. The whole family would be waiting for me on the other side of the glass panel. Look, there he is, how tall he's got, what nice clothes he has. Sitting in the car on the way home, I'd hand out presents, passing round a small photo of my new girlfriend.

The only thing that worried me about the army was the fire. Rafael had told me about an exercise in which you had to run through burning napalm. Everybody had to do it. I tried to visualize it as I lay in bed before I fell asleep. Friend after friend disappeared through the flames, until it was my turn. Come on, Jacob, I thought. Everyone can do it. Maybe it isn't even like normal fire; maybe it's a bit like that waterfall in the magic castle at Liseberg Amusement Park that you pass through without getting wet. But not even in my imagination did I succeed. I stood as if frozen to the spot, staring at the flames.

'By six votes to four Ben-Gurion's argument won the day,' said Sanna Grien, and wrote 6–4 on the blackboard.

She stood in front of the class with a cardigan neatly tied around her shoulders, along with a sheaf of multicoloured paper in her hand. She related that 250 guests were waiting at the museum in Tel Aviv, where Ben-Gurion was to announce the birth of the new state. They had been told to keep the ceremony secret. Otherwise there was a risk that the British would stop everything. They thought it was too early for a declaration of independence. So did the Americans, who had warned that payments would be stopped if they went ahead. No weapons would arrive if there was war.

Ben-Gurion wasn't about to delay for a second. Two thousand years of waiting was enough. It was now or never. At exactly four o'clock he would read the speech, the last details of which had been finalized by a man named Sharef in a building on the other side of the city.

When the clock approached half-past three, Sharef realized that he'd forgotten to arrange transport to the museum. He ran down to the street and stopped a car. After a long period of persuasion, the driver let him in. On their way they were pulled over for speeding. The driver panicked. The car was borrowed and, besides that, he had no driving licence. Sharef waved his document, explaining to the police that they were jeopardizing a historic mission. At one minute to four they arrived.

Reading from her piece of paper, Sanna said that it would be twenty years before Sharef was given an important post in an Israeli government.

Jonathan Friedkin tapped me on the thigh. He had the same type of skin as Bernie, his father: light with small brown freckles, like the outside of an overripe banana. I knew he was unhappy about his skin. The freckles were at their greatest density on his fingers and when he talked to girls he always held his hands behind his back or put them in his pockets.

'Look,' he said, and opened his left hand.

In his palm lay a completely black cassette. Even the wheels in the holes were black. Jonathan claimed he'd been given it by his relative in the USA. This relative had both an indoor and an outdoor pool. He had very special contacts in the music business and that was how he'd managed to get hold of the exclusive original recordings that Jonathan now held in his hand. I didn't believe a word of it.

'Give me three and you can borrow it.'

'Two,' I replied.

To my surprise, Jonathan accepted the offer without protest. He gratefully took the two pieces of strawberry chewing gum which I smuggled to him under the desk. His denim jacket hung over the chair behind him; he stuffed them down into one of the breast pockets without turning around.

A while later, he nudged me again. 'Has your mum's boss moved into your house now?'

I was surprised by the question. Luckily, I wasn't lost for words. Afterwards I was proud of myself. I'd tell Mum that Jonathan had asked, but that I'd denied it. She'd be pleased and say that she knew I was good at keeping secrets.

'That's what my dad says anyway.'

He'd turned to a fresh page in his notebook and wrote his name several times along the top line. He pressed his pencil hard against the paper as he wrote. The letters stood upright. None of them were larger or smaller than any others and they were all connected by diagonal lines that were equal in length. His signature looked as if it had been signed by someone who was seven years old and in love with his teacher.

'He sleeps on the sofa in the living room,' I said.

I wasn't sure if this was a lie too. Mum had made up a bed for Ingemar on the sofa. They had both said that it would be best if he slept there for the time being. Mirra had seen him in Mum's bed one night when she'd woken up and been frightened, but that didn't mean that he went up there every night.

Before Jonathan had time to say anything else, Miss Judith stood up behind her desk and cleared her throat, looking in our direction. Speaking with a calm voice, she said we'd be sent to the rabbi if we didn't stop disturbing the class. Then she sat down again. Sanna Grien adjusted her cardigan around her shoulders before turning around. In large letters, she wrote down the names of all the ministers in Israel's first government on the blackboard.

Instead of tapping the serving spoon against the edge of the plate, Grandma smoothed away the food remains with her thumb. Afterwards, she held the spoon up to the lamp, breathed out over its curved back and polished it.

'Pure quality,' she said.

The chicken we were served was thin and had knobbly skin. Lumps of congealed fat were lodged between the ribs at the back of its ribcage. I looked at my bit and it looked back at me imploringly, as if it knew that no one really wanted to have anything to do with it. Take me, it said, I'll do anything.

Ingemar had taste, Grandma stated. He could distinguish class from *drek*. Where had he got this amazing cutlery from? Maybe he'd bought it on one of his trips abroad. Or been given it as a present by a distinguished colleague. That's what happened in the business world, she explained. You continually gave one another expensive gifts to show your appreciation.

I quickly ate up the meat, then began to gnaw on the gristle. The bits next to the bone were the best. On Mum's chicken they were so tasty you had to eat the hard white bits too. On Mondays, there were usually leftovers of *shabbat* chicken in the fridge; on other days, I had difficulty finding anything particularly inspiring to eat when I got home. There was bread in the freezer, but nothing apart from cheese to put on it. Sometimes we had sausages at home, but they were usually kosher sausages. Apart from their shape, they had little in common with what normal people referred to as sausages. Just because the sausages weren't made of pork, the manufacturers assumed that nothing from the usual sausage recipe need apply. They thought they could add whatever they wanted – anything that couldn't be used in any other dish. Give it to the Jewish kids; they think that sausages are supposed to taste that way. Throw in whatever the hell you want. It never really felt like a meal when we were given sausages at our children's parties. It felt more like an experiment, as if the adults wanted to see if it was really possible to get small children to be happy with a meal whose main ingredients were vinegar and garlic powder.

Maybe that was the difference between our God and the Christian one. Their God had children. He understood that you have to go the extra mile when you're dealing with kids. That was why they got Christmas presents, Easter eggs and sausages that were spiced using a degree of discernment.

Our only equivalent was the bags of sweets we were given in the synagogue once a year, at Simchat Torah. There was always an unusual selection of goodies inside: a small packet of raisins, some peanuts, a mandarin. What was a mandarin doing in a collection of sweets?

I suspected that the unfortunate bags of sweets were part of our Eastern European heritage. Just like the sweaty cheese sandwiches we were given for Saturday *kiddush*. Only people from Eastern Europe could invent something like a perspiring sandwich. All of the old people in the congregation were from Eastern Europe. The rest of their culture had been exterminated in wars and persecution; only the food had survived. They had given their children Swedish forenames to blend in and they had pruned their surnames to the point of unrecognizability, but they retained their food. They could compromise with their identity, not their dried-out chickens and their sour vegetables. The very fact that, after all the tragedies, there still existed a living Eastern European Jewish food tradition at the end of the twentieth century was a historical triumph. It also contradicted the theory of evolution.

One thing I'd been wondering about was whether there was any connection between the standard of Jewish food and the fact that so much of our religion was to do with not eating. Don't eat pork; don't eat shellfish; don't eat milk with meat; use a very broad definition of the terms 'milk' and 'meat'. I had noticed how important it was to religious people to demonstrate that they could abstain from their dietary needs. This was particularly the case for family heads with rabbinical ambitions. Such as Papa Moysowich. At Passover, when we'd waited for hours and all that remained before the food was served was that he read a final short prayer, he was keen to demonstrate what worldly nonsense he regarded hunger to be. He certainly didn't care about such unnecessary complaints as malnourishment. He had all the time in the world. He could afford a slow digression, a poorly considered reflection or a long-winded pedagogical explanation to some child who thought that the encouragment to be curious (go ahead and ask, kids: Jewish culture is based on questioning; there are no silly questions) was meant literally.

Mirra finished her meal first. She asked if she could leave the table and hurried to put her plate in the dishwasher before she went back to the book that she'd left in the garden. Her choice of literature was an unceasing source of pride to our older relatives: exclusively books about the Holocaust; the testimonies of little girls, real and imaginary, in hiding or on the run, infatuated with a handsome *goy* boy who, from one day to the next, doesn't want to have anything to do with her, featuring a beloved kitten which the Nazis cold-bloodedly take away from her after they've seized her family.

Grandma cleared away my plate, then told me to remain seated at the table while she got her handbag. A scent of lipstick and leather gloves wafted into the air when it was opened. She dug around inside, removing her glasses case, her tram card and the latest edition of *Expressen*'s TV guide. I didn't understand why she was so determined to take it with her. TV guides were for people who had to choose which programmes they wanted to watch. Grandma watched everything. She couldn't bring herself to believe that anything on TV was bad. She thought that all the men on TV were good-looking, including politicians and the local newsreaders. Her TV evenings didn't come to an end until her neck gave out. When that happened, her head fell over the back of her chair, thin snoring sounds came from her nose and her neck looked as if it was about to snap. It was possible to pull the skin of her cheeks so far down that the edges met underneath her chin without waking her.

Grandpa was different. He divided up everything that was on TV into two categories: Jews and anti-Semites. Ingrid Bergman was Jewish. Greta Garbo was an anti-Semite. The TV news programme *Rapport* was slightly more anti-Semitic than the TV news programme *Aktuellt*. Pianists were Jews, as well as shopkeepers. Italians were Jews, as were Danes, and singers with thick, curly hair. The footballer Glenn Hysén was a Jew when he played for IFK Gothenburg, an anti-Semite when he played for Sweden. Sports reporters – anti-Semites. Actors in Eastern European films – anti-Semites. Actors in Gothenburg-produced TV drama series – deeply committed anti-Semites.

Grandpa's mornings were identical every day of the week. He got up at four o'clock, positioned his chair next to the kitchen window, put his hands on his knees, moved his eyes to the left, then to the right, then up, then down. He claimed this exercise improved his eyesight. I joined him one morning, when he and Grandma had spent the night at our house. I sat next to him in the kitchen, with my duvet, and bit my fingers in order to avoid falling back to sleep. Grandpa closed his eyes when he had finished his workout.

'What are you doing now?' I asked.

'Talking to my mother,' he said.

I asked what they talked about and he said it was everyday things mostly. What he'd had for dinner. Something he'd seen on TV. Grandpa was five years old when his family had come to Gothenburg in the 1920s. They had fled from their village, through Czechoslovakia, all the way to the Baltic States. In Riga they'd climbed aboard a ship that they thought would take them to America. Instead, they ended up sharing a flat in the Gothenburg district of Haga together with another Jewish family. At the beginning of October every year, they had to go to the police Aliens Bureau on Spannmålsgatan and apply for renewed residency status.

Sometimes they were met by thorough clerks who examined their file with expressionless faces. Sometimes they encountered talkative jokers who made a show of the meeting, who called in colleagues as an audience and held their noses as long as they remained in the building.

Grandpa's father worked as a door-to-door salesman. One year, the police authorities notified him that they'd found discrepancies in his accounting. They announced that he was to be deported, as was his wife. Grandpa's parents appealed against the decision, on the basis that they'd lived in the country for fifteen years, that their sons were doing national service for Sweden and that the German annexation of Czechoslovakia had made the situation for Jews there even more dangerous than before.

Grandpa was doing his national service at Army Barracks 116 in Halmstad and couldn't come to Gothenburg to say farewell. His father was shot a week after his arrival in Prague. His mother ended up in Theresienstadt concentration camp, but she survived and was reunited with her children after the war. A few months later, she was picking flowers in Delsjön Park, in the east of Gothenburg, when she was run over by the No. 5 tram.

Grandma pulled a Double Dime chocolate bar out of her bag. Dime was one of the best types of chocolate in the world, she said. By far superior to the Plopp chocolate bar, for instance. What *scheiss*. You took two bites, then it was finished. The outer coating was a layer as thin as paper. You got heartburn from the cheap caramel mixture inside. Grandma screwed up her face in distaste before clearing her throat, as though her oesophagus had become sore just by talking about it.

I gnawed the chocolate off first, then started on the toffee. Grandma thought that you should suck a Dime bar, as if it were a sweet. It isn't just that it's tastier that way, she argued, it lasts longer too. I had tried to explain that it was difficult. You couldn't always control your teeth and if they'd decided to demolish something in your mouth, then there was nothing you could do. She said she understood, but when she heard the sound of crunching between my teeth, she still used to look at me with dissatisfied eyes. But this time she just sat opposite me in silence, tapping her nails impatiently against the table. She asked how Dad was. I said he'd been in quite a good mood the last time we'd met. '*God zei dank*,' said Grandma, still beating an impatient rhythm against the wooden surface of the table with her nails. After a while, she got up and wiped the crumbs from the table. She cupped one hand under the table, while with the other she brushed them into it from the table's edge. She asked what Dad and I had done; if we'd been at Mame and Grandad's. When I said yes, she clasped the hand holding the crumbs into a fist, then angled her head upwards. 'What did she say this time?'

I thought it looked as though Grandma had a hint of a smile on her red-painted lips. I balanced the chair against the wall behind me. It didn't matter what I answered. Grandma knew what Mame said nowadays when I helped her dry the dishes. During the weeks that had passed since Dad had moved out and Ingemar had moved in, Mame had managed to spread her suspicions to most of the congregation. Mame was sure that Grandma and Grandpa had known for a long time that Mum had embarked on an affair with her boss. She thought that they'd helped her keep it secret. She would never forgive Grandma and Grandpa for sharing the same table as her at my bar mitzvah, for having sung and celebrated, while simultaneously knowing what was about to happen.

'The same as usual,' I said, and let the chair fall back down to the floor.

Grandma stood in front of me for a while, then walked over to the kitchen sink and brushed the crumbs from her hands. She turned the water on and washed her hands, while looking out into the garden. She dampened a cloth and rubbed the worktop in a jerky fashion, muttering that all of Mame's family were mad.

Up to this point Grandpa had been silent. He'd sat on his chair and eaten his own uniquely concocted dessert – a large dollop of marmalade in a teacup – in a calm and measured fashion, as if what Grandma and I had been talking about didn't concern him in the least. Now he eagerly scraped the teaspoon against the bottom of the cup. He told us about Mame's brother who wrote poetry and hadn't left his flat at Redbergsplatsen since the end of the 1960s. He related the story about one of her cousins who'd been to prison and about someone who'd married her own uncle.

Grandma pushed the dishcloth slowly around the hotplates on the cooker. She nodded as Grandpa talked, filling in the gaps in his stories. Both of them laughed when one of them mentioned a name they hadn't heard in a long while.

Outside it grew dark. Grandma put her hand to her mouth when she saw that the time was almost half-past eight, realizing that she'd missed several hours of TV entertainment. She rushed into the living room, while Grandpa and I put the tea on.

At the same time in Israel, there was a heated debate surrounding the song 'Shir Habatlanim', which earlier that year had represented the country in the Eurovision Song Contest. The lyrics dealt with an unemployed slacker who didn't get out of bed until late in the morning. Religious groups were opposed to the song's indolent message. The Minister of Culture had threatened to resign.

Sweden had, somewhat surprisingly, entered the debate by means of record company executive Bert Karlsson, who, during the summer, had recorded a cover version of the song. 'Hoppa Hulle', as it was known in Sweden, attained very modest sales figures, but the recording was still regarded as a welcome easing of tension in Swedish-Israeli relations. At least among Gothenburg's Jewish contingent.

For them, relations with the Swedish Eurovision establishment had been plagued by mistrust ever since the 1978 contest, when Sweden was the only nation to give Israel and Izhar Cohen's winning entry, 'A-Ba-Ni-Bi', no points. Admittedly, what some people – specifically Grandpa and perhaps a few others – claimed was not true: namely, that *all* other countries had given Israel maximum points on that occasion. But no points for such an upbeat disco classic was bad enough, and it was immediately associated with the anti-Israel feeling that was assumed to permeate the whole of Swedish society.

Emotions were running high the following year, when Israel itself hosted the competition. For my parents and their friends, it was like watching their child go off into the city on her own for the very first time. One moment they were proud; the next they were filled with regrets. She isn't ready for it. She won't be able

40

to handle it. Maybe she should have kept on doing simpler tasks for a little longer. Like winning wars in the desert, for instance. Or gunning down Egyptians while they're still reading through the instruction manual for their new Soviet jets. Safe things, things she's familiar with. Let others handle the entertainment in the meantime.

The broadcast began with a sequence of desolate pictures of Jerusalem that was far too long. A sad flute played in the background, while solitary buses drove past. The next problem was the stage decor. It consisted of three rings which revolved around one another. While perhaps geometrically interesting, it seemed to belong more to the reception area of a research laboratory than to the biggest European entertainment event of the year.

Contributing to the tense atmosphere in front of the TV were the depressing advance reports that had leaked out about this year's Israeli entry. The country had apparently abandoned its winning upbeat-tempo format of the previous year and had now dusted off some high-flown quasi-religious effort which had previously been regarded as being too poor for international competition. The favourite instead was France, which as usual had submitted a strong ballad, as well as Austria, with their ingratiating entry, 'Heute in Jerusalem'. The outsider was West Germany. Their 'Dschinghis Khan' was a spectacularly choreographed performance about the controversial Mongol ruler, which drew enormous applause when it featured as the ninth entry of the evening.

Then it was Israel's turn.

I crept as close to the screen as I could without being told off. I experienced a mysterious ache in my stomach at the sight of the woman who sang the first verse, accompanied only by a piano and a guitar. She had a flower-patterned dress, a fringe tucked behind her ears, and three boyfriends. At least that was how I interpreted her relation to the smiling but, happily

41

enough, not too attractive men in braces, bow ties and beige trousers who soon accompanied her on stage.

My love grew throughout the performance. With every verse an instrument was added to the simple and catchy melody, until it really began to get going after the third chorus. The song increased in intensity until you couldn't believe it was possible to go any further, but then they redoubled their efforts, with all four of them singing in unison, while the conductor gesticulated ever more wildly, until the song finally exploded in an exceptional crescendo.

Not even the Swedes, usually swayed by current political issues, could resist it. 'Hallelujah' collected a twelve-pointer from Stockholm, as well as an additional five of these from, among others, the United Kingdom and Portugal. Gaining ten points in the last round of voting, Israel passed Spain's Betty Missiego and her sedentary children's choir. The miracle had been repeated. In Spanish bars there were grumbles about the Jewish world conspiracy. On our upper floor, Dad danced into the toilet door, making a crack in it that would never be repaired.

When Grandad had finished reading his letter, Ingemar took him into the kitchen. Grandad subsequently came out of the kitchen bearing a fully loaded plate and with a confused expression on his face. He sat down next to me. I wanted to lift up his arm, put it over my shoulder and then press myself against his stomach.

'She hasn't got long to go now.'

Grandad shovelled food into his mouth. He made it look tasty when he ate. He didn't think that you'd eaten enough if there was any trace of food left on your plate. When I was small, I used to be allowed to sit on his knee at the end of a meal. Both holding a piece of bread, we would help each other to mop up the remaining drops of gravy from the porcelain.

'Ten minutes is enough,' he said. 'Is that too much to ask? She hasn't done you any harm.'

His jaws were masticating, creating deep valleys under his ears. I thought he was being unfair. I used to go and visit Mame when I went up to town. Not every time perhaps, but I had been there on several occasions. Each time I'd hurried through the entrance while staring at the floor, then gone up the stairs and along the corridor. Mame's room was on the second floor. She had the circular chest of drawers that used to be in the flat, as well as all the photos. No one was allowed to look at them. Once when I got there, she was asleep in her blue armchair. Her lower lip was jutting out and her hairline was shining with perspiration. When she awoke and saw me, her eyes were filled with a radiant light for a few tenths of a second, before her system got going properly. 'Josef?' she asked.

Her cheeks grew red as she realized her mistake. Afterwards there was a silent disappointment, which lasted until she fell asleep again.

The first time Dad was in Israel without his parents was July 1967. After having begun the summer with the astoundingly swift victory in the Six Day War, the country found itself in the grip of military and religious euphoria. Between them and their worst enemy, Egypt, Israel now had a 3,728-square-mile buffer zone. To the only remaining part of the Temple, Jews now had free access for the first time in more than 2,000 years.

Dad worked in a plastics factory on a kibbutz. Someone had a Volkswagen van and one night they drove out into the desert. They climbed up to the ruins of Masada in the darkness, saw the sun rise over the sand dunes, then climbed down before the sun's rays, shining at the height of summer, made further physical exertion impossible. Before having breakfast, they swam in the nearby Dead Sea.

The van stopped outside a hovel on the slope of a hill. Behind a counter, lustrous juicy lamb was turning on a spit. Dad couldn't take his eyes off it. There were vegetables in a bowl on a table. You could take as much as you liked. Dad jammed his pitta bread full before he handed it over to the stall owner, who then pushed meat down into the bread that was already stuffed to bursting.

It was the most delicious sandwich Dad had ever eaten. He told me about it one evening when he came into my room. He was really only coming in to say goodnight, but he remained on my bed, in his suit trousers, shirt and shoes, with his arm tucked under my head. I told him that I didn't think he could call a kebab a sandwich. A kebab was a meal. A sandwich wasn't really a meal. It was halfway between a snack and a proper dinner.

Dad said, 'Jacob, it's a sandwich if bread is one of the main

45

ingredients. Especially when, as in this case, the bread surrounds the rest of the food.'

He looked up towards the ceiling, then started listing all the other sandwiches that he thought deserved a mention. Those that Mame made with salmon and mayonnaise. Sandwiches with chopped liver, either with or without egg. Then he remembered gherkins; if you had gherkins on a sandwich it immediately counted as one of his favourites. The same went for tuna, and the Reuben. Oh, my God, the Reuben. Imagine that: he'd almost forgotten about the Reuben.

'It's an American classic,' he said. 'Possibly the world's most famous sandwich.'

At least three nationalities claimed the credit for inventing it. The Swiss believed that the cheese indicated that they were behind it. The Russians pointed to the dark bread, which they felt was in their favour. Within Jewish culture, we believed that the Old Testament forename after which the sandwich was called was sufficient evidence of its origins. The opposing sides' main argument against our claim was that the popular sandwich contained both cheese and meat, so therefore wasn't kosher. Dad didn't think this was an especially convincing argument: maybe Reuben didn't subscribe to the laws of *kashrut*. Israel was built by secular Jews; they were possibly also capable of creating a tasty sandwich. At the deli where Dad, together with Mum, had first tasted the Reuben a few years earlier, the conflict had been resolved by the owner in a way everyone could agree upon. 'Where does the Reuben come from?' asked an article cut out from the newspaper that the owner had stuck up above the till. Directly beneath it, he had written: 'Straight from heaven, that's where.'

My best sandwich memory was at this point only a week or so old, which was probably the reason why the topic had come up in the first place. I was going to the congregation building for a bar mitzvah lesson, but had just missed the bus at the stop outside school. It was raining and I was considering crossing the road to take the bus in the opposite direction, travelling home the long way round, when I saw the headlights of Dad's car coming round the corner.

It was warm inside the car and it smelled nice from Dad's new cologne. He kept casting meaningful looks at a thick foil-wrapped package that lay on top of the glove compartment. Inside the silver wrapping were two double-decker sandwiches, made from soft white bread, that were cut into triangles. Strong cheese and large amounts of sliced cucumber had been pushed in between the pieces of bread. I had finished eating before we'd even made it on to the motorway. I remember that we talked about that special phenomenon, the way the sandwich that you hardly care about at home can be completely unforgettable somewhere else.

There were two boxes containing his belongings in the store room. Inside them were old winter clothes, a small *menorah* and a worn leather folder crammed full of school exercise books and reports.

There was a well-preserved learn-to-read book. A football poster he'd made himself. There was also his large 'SAY IT LOUD' poster, which had once been pinned up in the congregation bar. It had small holes where the drawing pins had been.

The boxes contained a passport issued in 1981: height 1.76 metres; eyes brown. A large pipe and a watch that had stopped. A chain with a gigantic Star of David.

There were faded black and white photos. A picture taken in profile at the harbour, featuring Dad with sideburns, a suede jacket and a woolly polo-neck jumper. There was one picture of him with a happy smile sitting in the driver's seat of a car. Another of him wearing a settler's cap and denim shorts on a tank at sunset.

There were newspaper cuttings in a plastic folder: Begin and Sadat reach late-night agreement... New protests outside the Soviet Trade Centre... A group of doctors at Sahlgrenska Hospital have discovered a brand-new method to... Engaged, married, newborns.

His doctoral thesis, bound in soft red covers. A bundle of congratulation cards with signatures.

A dark-blue pocket diary for the last year. Planned meetings. Birthdays. Personal reflections jotted down in the lower corner. Whole days' plans crossed out with harsh strokes of the pen.

There were no entries on or after the Friday that his colleague had called.

Mame didn't stop talking the whole way to the meeting. About her father, whom she said was a genius, about her mother, who had long legs, and about her own phenomenal gift for languages. 'Can you imagine, Coybele, that I still speak Russian, after all these years, and isn't it tragic, Coybele, that I will never be able to use my German again? Did you know that I was once mistaken for an Austrian, that's how pure and beautiful my language was, but I will never speak their words again, as I'm sure you understand, and the Russians are even worse: I do *not* trust Gorbachev, a false smile, pogroms, anti-Semites, the Gulag, Auschwitz, and *bist* you really *sicher* you *nicht in Österreich* is born *meine Fräulein, fantastich, unglaublich.*'

Dad had told us that Mame's family came from the Ukraine. Her father was a deeply religious man who was unhappy with his job as a travelling salesman. To escape the competition he travelled northwards. On a train between Königsberg and Stettin he shared a compartment with a group of Swedish salesmen. When they had got off the train he found a long list of suppliers and customers that they had left behind. He read names such as Isaksson, Abrahamsson and Josefsson, which led him to believe that the country they came from was teeming with pious Jews.

When we arrived at the meeting hall, things had already begun. Mame pulled out two chairs for us in the back row. She took off both her shawls and placed them on her knee. She greeted acquaintances with a long funereal nod.

The discussion was led by Katzman's cousin. She sat with Zaddinksky at a small table facing the rows of chairs. There was a notepad on the table, at which she sometimes glanced. Rectangular windows covered the long sides of the meeting hall. Cars looking for a parking space could be seen between the concrete pillars of the multi-storey car park across the street. Between the windows were portraits of old rabbis. One wore a large square hat and looked like a Catholic bishop.

The Nightingale had stood up in the front row. He had round cheeks which hung down on either side of his face. I didn't know what his real name was. He was the loudest singer in the synagogue. He sang complicated melodies which continued long after everyone else had finished. Sometimes I thought I could see a slight disappointment in his eyes that there was no one who could follow him to the furthest reaches of tonality. Perhaps he felt alone in his vocal superiority. Perhaps he'd had a rival when he was young, someone with an almost equally beautiful voice who had pushed him to the limits of his ability. Then came the war and now there was nothing; he was surrounded by tone-deaf idiots, and the Yiddish choir was about to be disbanded, and now, on top of everything else, this art exhibition.

There was, he said, rolling up his shirt sleeves, just one way to describe what the Arts Council had allowed into the hall. Just one way: a work of degradation. That was what it should be called. Not a work of art. Not positive identity politics. A work of degradation. For five years he had been forced to bear it, he said, touching his chest where the star had been. He had promised his mother never to accept it again. Now he would have to see it as he went to his own *shul*, on the walls here among his own congregation!

I didn't know which side to support. The Nightingale was convincing, but I also felt sorry for Katzman's cousin. I had seen a little of the exhibition as I came in. Only a little, because Mame had held one hand in front of my eyes, pulling me along with the other. She said that I had to help her up the stairs; she couldn't bear to see the wretched display; she refused to look at it. The exhibition consisted mostly of paintings with slogans

50

written in bright colours: 'U R jew-nique!', 'U R b-jew-tiful!', 'No more h-jew-miliation!' The old people were furious about the flag which was suspended above the coffee machine. It was an ordinary Swedish flag, except that the cross had been replaced by the Star of David. The artists hadn't considered the unpleasant connotations a Star of David in yellow cloth might have for many members of the congregation.

The Nightingale walked back and forth between the chairs as he talked. He discussed the great progress that mankind had made since he was a child. He picked out the moon landings and the formation of the United Nations. He devoted a surprising amount of time to technological development. Then he raised his index finger and said that as far as we were concerned all those things didn't really matter. As far as we were concerned the state of Israel was the most important thing. 'Israel has made us strong,' he thundered. 'Israel has made us free. We have a life insurance policy today. We can say no today. Therefore, friends, I have to say, if we are to have a flag in the lobby – bring forth the flag of Israel instead.'

An explosion of applause filled the room. Walking sticks hammered against the floor. Mame stood up and clapped her hands. She used to do that in front of the TV too, which had disturbed me considerably when I was younger. 'They can't see you,' I used to say. 'Sit down.' 'No, I think they're playing brilliantly.' She stood up for the entirety of Wilander's final against Lendl in the 1985 French Open. And yet she didn't even like Wilander. She thought he spat too much. Björn Borg was better. He never spat. He swallowed – 'like a gentleman'. On that occasion it wasn't only me. Everyone wanted her to sit down, but Mame just turned up the volume, saying that she thought it was idiotic that they started again every time they reached six games. They could at least play until they reached ten. 'Or they could set a timer, play for an hour and the one who's won the most points would be the champion. It's crazy. Look, now he's spitting again.'

The Nightingale had put his hand on Katzman's cousin's shoulder. He explained that he'd been a very close friend of her mother's. He knew that she too had been exposed to the horrors of the Holocaust. She was a wonderful woman and he could only commiserate that she was no longer among us. If she were still alive, perhaps she might have been able to make her child see sense. Perhaps she would have said, 'My beloved little daughter, one shouldn't laugh at the sufferings of other people.' It was this that was the great danger. That the witnesses were disappearing. Soon there wouldn't be anyone left who could relate what had happened. People who'd learned nothing from history would have free rein. Was that the future he would be leaving to his grandchildren? It worried him, he said, and he didn't stop talking about it until Katzman's cousin stood up, saying in a loud voice that her mother wasn't dead at all. She had seen the exhibition and she liked it.

A silence descended over the room for a while. The Nightingale rubbed his earlobe, then shrugged his shoulders. If her mother was still alive, why hadn't she got in touch? 'Is that how one treats old friends?' he said. Finally, Zaddinsky asked Ethel Zaft down in the corner to say something about the meetings for older people coming up in the autumn.

'*Meine* hands, look at *meine* hands, Jacob. Look how they shake, look at them.'

We were sitting on the upper floor of Bräutigam's café. Old ladies ate pastries with forks. Mineral water was poured into glasses, emitting a peaceful fizz.

I had been given a Coca-Cola and I stirred the ice cubes at the bottom of the glass with a straw. An old man played the piano further down the room. Mame turned round occasionally and stared at him with threatening eyes. How could they let such a *putz* touch the keyboard? It hurt her just listening to it. She had difficulty listening to music in general now that she could no longer play herself. No tunes would ever come from her fingers again; that path to pleasure was closed to her. She couldn't sleep at night. She lay awake, in the blue bedroom, with her eyes sore from the street lights which shone in through the blinds, while her ears winced from the screeching of the dawn's first trams. She blamed herself. That's what you did as a mother. He had been sensitive even as a child. He had needed someone who understood him.

I directed the straw at the hollow craters of the ice cubes and sucked up the cola that had collected there. Mame placed a hand on either side of her cup. Her tea bag had lost its small paper tag and it floated just below the surface, trailing its white thread behind it. I wanted to ask her what had happened to Dad at work on the day that his colleague had called, but I couldn't think of a good way to phrase the question.

'He could have had anyone,' said Mame in a low voice. 'The entire congregation wanted him. He wouldn't listen to me. It was as if he was bewitched, Coybele. As if he was bewitched, I say.'

She drank her tea slowly, in short, sharp slurps. Every time she put down her cup she looked at me and nodded, as if to underline everything she'd just said. When the cup was empty she got up, saying that she was going to the toilet. I was to come with her and stand guard, she explained. She didn't dare lock the door. The door could get jammed. 'Here you are,' she said, rifling through her coat pocket. 'Have a Plopp bar.'

In the queue for the toilets she told me that a long time ago a Yiddish woman had played the café's piano. It had been a delight to sit there in those days. She had a son who was a few years younger than Dad, 'a little *kacker* this high,' she said, and measured with her hand about three feet above the floor, 'but a genius'.

Mame continued to talk about the pianist's talented son even after she'd entered the toilet. He had worked in Paris and now he had a position with the Finance Minister. One day – *baruch hashem* – he would perhaps sit in the government, 'and there, Coybele,' I heard her say behind the closed toilet door, 'there you will see what knowledge can do. With knowledge the smallest can rise all the way to the top.'

54

I asked Aunt Irene for a cigarette. She smoked a brand with yellow and brown stripes on the packet, which perfectly suited her new status, now that she'd taken early retirement. Getting her pension had been a great success for her. She thereby carried on a proud family tradition from her mother and aunts. Sometimes it felt as though she looked at Mirra and me in order to discover which of us would carry the torch on through the twenty-first century.

It had been a long time since I last smoked and the cigarette tasted strange, but it went down fine with the help of a glass of whisky which Aunt Irene had poured for me. She topped us up regularly, especially Grandad, which I guessed was her way of attempting to forestall his aim of making this visit as brief as possible.

'*L'chaim*,' she said, and raised her glass.

While Grandad was heart-stricken at having to visit Mum and Ingemar's house, Aunt Irene had gone to the other extreme and was wildly animated. She tapped her cigarettes excitedly against the clear glass ashtray, interrogating me about everything she saw around her. Who was that in the photo? Where had they bought that chest of drawers? Were there more photos anywhere? What had they paid for the house?

I looked at the ashtray, which had been given to Mum by some relative. It had a map of Europe engraved at the bottom. Ingemar had noticed it the first time he visited us. After dinner I had found myself alone with him in the living room. Mum was doing something in the kitchen and every time the floorboards creaked I hoped she was on her way back in to us. I was ashamed of my inability to think of anything to say. He asked how I was doing at school. I said things were going well. I asked about the Swedish Premier League. He said he supported Hammarby. We were able to spin out two or three more sentences on the subject of football before all fell quiet again. I began to imagine that my swallowing was audible. Do people really swallow this much normally? I wondered. I had never had problems swallowing before, but now my mouth was suddenly full of saliva that I had to get down my throat at any cost. All the time Ingemar sat holding the ashtray in his hand. 'It's very pretty,' he said at one point, 'don't you think?'

When Mum finally came back from the kitchen, I pulled it over to my side of the table. What was it that made this particular ashtray so beautiful? Was it the grooves in the glass? Or the map of Europe? Maybe that was it: that the person who'd made the ashtray had been able to fit the whole of Europe into that tiny space. Because it looked almost exactly like Europe.

The ashtray was one of the few things that remained from our terraced house. Almost everything else had been thrown out when we moved. The green sofa had been taken to the rubbish dump. Aunt Laura's paintings were removed from the walls, then put in plastic bin bags. Ingemar had made a list of every room in the house, with an arrow pointing at the name of the person whose responsibility it was to empty it.

The store room was my task, but I nagged Mum until she agreed to help me. I hoped that coming into contact with all our old things would affect her in some way; get her to remember some event, something he used to say, become a bit sorrowful maybe, and run her fingers slowly over his old fur hat. I pushed photos into her field of vision, along with one of his jumpers I knew she had liked. She looked at it, smiled, then said, 'Save that one if you want, darling. It's up to you,' and moved on to the next shelf.

The circumcision had made a mess of Katzman's cock. When the foreskin had been cut away the top had pulled itself inwards. It hid among the folds of skin, shy and embarrassed, as if unable to greet the outside world without its protective sheath.

I looked around the classroom and realized that I knew most things about my male friends' genitals. They were all quite similar.

It was different in regular school. The shower after gym in my first year was the first time I had seen a collection of Protestant penises. I couldn't get as clear a visual impression as I wanted to because our teacher had made us wear rubber caps with a plastic visor that steamed up in front of our eyes, but what I had seen was impressive. The wide variety made for a dramatic contrast to the uniformity I was used to from the Jewish congregation. I guessed this was a result of the fact that my friends and I had all been circumcised by the same *mohel*. Everyone apart from Katzman that is, because when he was due to be circumcised our ordinary *mohel* was ill. They'd had to summon some old man from Stockholm, who arrived tired and dazed after five hours in the car.

It would never have happened in the USA. They had *mohels* everywhere. That was why everyone we knew loved the USA. I had noticed that, however much they protected and revered Israel, it was the USA they dreamed of. In the USA there were whole schools consisting only of Jews. Holiday resorts, businesses, suburbs. Yiddish words in everyday language. Bagel salesmen on street corners, and just about everywhere – *mohels*. There was a special heading in the *Yellow Pages* for *mohels*. Page after page of *mohels*.

In Sweden it was different. Here they just complained. They thought that circumcision was for barbarians. At any moment they would ban it completely. Dad and the other doctors in the congregation were continually having to publicly defend our tradition. Their task was to inform people of the hygienic advantages of circumcision and emphasize its central position in our faith. And – in my opinion, most important of all – keep Katzman's genitalia far from the media spotlight.

Katzman's upper body was covered in a claret turtleneck jumper that slid up and exposed the lower part of his back when he leaned over his desk. It was his turn to give a talk, but he had to wait because Zaddinsky had come into the classroom, together with a girl with light-brown hair.

Miss Judith told us to be quiet. Zaddinsky spat out his chewing gum in the waste-paper basket next to the teacher's desk, then extended his arm towards the girl. She took a step forward, pushed her fringe back behind her ear and told us that her name was Alexandra.

She was from the Soviet Union. I thought the Soviet Jews were exciting. They had to suffer forcible incarceration in mental hospitals, work camps and police violence. For one year in Hebrew school we'd had the Jews of the Soviet Union as our theme. Before we broke up for the summer holidays we staged our interpretation of the Dymshits–Kuznetsov hijacking affair in the meeting hall. Sixteen people around a table on the stage. Low voices. A steady dripping from a broken pipe in the ceiling. I played Kuznetsov and had just worked out a brilliant way to escape. We would pretend to be on our way to a wedding, then buy every ticket on a domestic flight between Leningrad and a city with an unpronounceable name. Once we were up in the air my pilot co-conspirator (Sanna Grien) would take the controls and fly the plane to Sweden.

Miss Judith prompted from a chair to one side of the front row. The parents applauded every completely delivered line.

58

It was all organized in minute detail, but nothing worked out as planned. Before we had left the airport my entire group was arrested by two brutal policemen (Jonathan Friedkin and Jaël Sopher). The pilot and I were sentenced to death. In the second act, our sentence was reduced after pressure from the West (Adam Katzman and Ariella Moysowich).

Protests might help: that was the message of the piece. For those people who hadn't been able to work that out, it perhaps became clear after the play, when every participant stood at the front of the stage, reading it out from their own individual piece of creased paper.

And we signed petitions to the embassy of the Soviet Union. We drew pictures and wrote encouraging greetings. Brave volunteers travelled over there with secret letters. Mum and Dad had done that once. They'd smuggled in prayer books. They'd heard strange clicks when they lifted the receiver of the phone in their hotel room. There was a photo from the trip: a snowy bridge, Mum in a beige coat with an enormous collar, Dad in a long coat and fur hat.

Alexandra was given the seat beside Sanna Grien. Miss Judith nodded at Katzman, who got up and confidently strode towards the teacher's desk, carrying a large sheaf of paper in his hand. I stared at Alexandra's neck and hoped I could fall in love with her. The other girls in the class didn't bear thinking about. Maybe because I knew them too well. Maybe because they were too prissy. At least, that's what Mum said about their mothers. Mirra and I had been sitting on Mum's bed one evening when she was clearing out her wardrobe. She picked at her old clothes, frowning in an expression of suspicion bordering on hate. 'Did I really wear this?' she said. 'I must have been mad. It's the sort of thing that Fanny Grien would own.' Of all the sneering comments she poured out at her old clothes, it soon became apparent that 'Fanny Grien' was the very worst. It wasn't just a name, it was shorthand for curtains, small cars, part-time work, charity meetings with the girls on Wednesday, kosher food on Thursday afternoon, and I saw that Mum enjoyed pushing the tainted clothes deep down into the black bin bag.

I was a little afraid of Sanna Grien's parents. Her father once heard me say to Sanna that I didn't think that Magic Morris Meyer was a real magician. All he could do was blow up balloons and twist them into different animals. He performed at every children's party the congregation organized and he did the same things every time. It was skilful, admittedly, but it wasn't magic. Sanna's father started grinning in the front seat. Could I explain how he did it, then? Had I tried to do it myself? Because he had, and he thought I should know that the balloons burst. There was nothing left of the balloons when normal people tried to turn them into animals. How anyone could get those thin damn balloons to stay in one piece, let alone combine them into one imaginative animal after the other, he really didn't know. And if something really couldn't be understood… then it was magic.

No, Mr Grien, you're wrong. In order for something to be called magic there has to be a sense of mystery; something which is hidden, or suddenly appears from nowhere; some form of surprise at least – and that was the last thing you could say that Meyer offered. I wish I had said that in their dark-blue Opel that day, but it didn't occur to me until much later.

After the lesson Miss Judith stopped me and told me to go and see the rabbi.

The door was open a few inches. I pushed it slowly, then stood there, slightly inside the doorway, without knowing what to do. The rabbi continued to work behind his desk paying me no attention. After a while he mumbled something which wasn't words, but at least suggested that he had noticed he was no longer alone in the room.

I sat down in the blue office chair and swivelled slightly from side to side. The office was so small it wasn't possible to spin round entirely. If I went too far to the right, I immediately banged my knees against the wall. If I went too far to the left, my feet got stuck on the bottom shelf of the bookcase.

The desk almost filled the room. On it were piles of prayer books, cut-out newspaper articles that lay with half their text hanging over the edge, small jars of aspirin that rolled about and scattered powder. In the middle of everything was a typewriter that the rabbi angrily assaulted with his index fingers. He had on round glasses and wore a white shirt and a black waistcoat. His chin sported a curly beard in which grey hairs stood out among the dark ones. Sometimes he pulled the paper out of the typewriter, then scrunched it up with one hand. He swore while he wrote. In English mostly – he was from Chicago and had been with us for five years without really learning Swedish. How could they expect him to have time to do everything? he muttered. Columns in the congregation's newsletter. Financial discussions with the Board of Trustees. Ecumenical gimmicks with priests and imams.

The telephone rang. The rabbi didn't answer. He gathered

61

together the pile of papers, banged the short ends against the desk and brushed aside a collection of brochures lying in the way of his stapler. It was only then that he became properly aware of my presence. He leaned over the desk, ruffled my hair, sank back, told me why he'd asked me to come and see him, and asked a few questions. Then the telephone rang again. The rabbi lifted the receiver, said, 'Later, Sarah darling, later,' hung up and asked the questions again, more slowly this time, using more Swedish words, as if the answers I'd just given him were so outlandish that they must have been based on a misunderstanding.

'Jay-cob…' He looked at me with concern as he spoke, then paused. 'I have to say…'

His wife rang him because they couldn't have any children. When I was studying for my bar mitzvah, I was often sent out into the corridor. I need a moment here Jay, he'd say. Then I would hear him through the door as he spoke with a gentle and understanding voice. 'Yes, Sarah. No, Sarah. I feel that way too, Sarah.'

'… in all my life… I don't think I've seen anyone…'

No children. What a scandal. A rabbi, Mr Weizmann, should have a kid suspended from each of his trouser legs, one clambering over the Torah scrolls and an unidentified number playing hide-and-seek in his beard.

'… so unaffected.'

The rabbi took off his glasses. He wiped them with the inside of his waistcoat and laughed to himself, more in confusion than in mirth, or so it sounded. He rested his elbows on the desk, then pressed his hands together in front of his nose. Having sat completely still for a while, he waved his hands forward and asked me if I knew what a rabbi actually was.

Unlike those he'd posed earlier, I wasn't prepared for this question. I gently kicked a square waste-paper basket, which tipped over underneath the desk. A grey plastic bag had been folded around its edge. Among the scrunched-up pieces of paper at the top, the core of a pear he'd eaten was visible.

'A rabbi, Jay,' he said, clasping his fingers together, 'is an ordinary guy who happens to know a bit about what's in the Torah. There's nothing holy about him. He doesn't have the power to forgive, like a priest does. He has no short cut to God. He has this –' he patted a book on the desk – 'and nothing else.' He shifted his gaze to the book, as if this was what he was speaking to now, and stroked the dust from the cover in careful, almost tender motions. 'Luckily enough, it goes a long way,' he said, 'maybe further than anyone can comprehend. But, amazing as it may be, not even this text can prepare you for all the difficulties you'll encounter the day you begin to work in a congregation. From the moment you step through the doors of a new synagogue, as well as every day thereafter, from early morning until late at night, new and *com-pletely* unexpected questions will come at you.'

He bent his fingers into claws and demonstrated with both hands what it looked like when you came at something.

'Now,' he said, then placed the book on top of two others before moving the entire pile a bit to the left, 'in a small congregation, when a conflict arises between people with whom many others have a strong relationship, they choose sides. They look for scapegoats and say things they don't mean. Call him, call her, persuade your father to go to the autumn party, ask your mother to stay at home on Rosh Hashanah and Yom Kippur. No, I tell them, it's not my business. But, Jay –' he stretched his arms in both directions, then leaned so far over the typewriter that I could feel the warmth of his breath – 'if an old bar mitzvah student needs help – then it is my business. If he has questions and doesn't know where to turn – then it is my business. If he, just once, is worried about what it'll be like to attend synagogue – then it is definitely my business. Understand?'

I nodded without being quite sure what he meant. He had

said his piece, I could see that, and now it was my turn. Whatever I wanted to say or ask — now I had my chance. But I couldn't think of anything.

Through the door I heard my classmates enter the corridor. The rabbi had sunk back down into his chair. He looked at me with a thoughtful expression, until he realized that he had a book that he wanted me to read. He reached over to the bookcase and paper tumbled down on to the floor, and before he'd found the book he was looking for, the phone rang again.

When Dad came home after having been away or having worked late, he usually ended up on his back on the sofa, with his head propped against the armrest. His legs would be folded and form a triangle with his thighs and the sofa cushion. Mirra and I came out in our pyjamas, taking turns to hang on to his lower legs. He swayed them from side to side, lifting them up so that we could slide all the way down to his stomach. I would lie there for as long as I could, pressing the large soft veins on his hand.

Sometimes, when they argued, Mum said that he was a cheapskate, but I didn't agree with her. Dad's relationship with money was more complicated than that. It concerned him. He felt bad having anything to do with it. He came up with different systems to help him to deal with it. He had folders and plastic files and pieces of paper containing calculations that were placed in the files, which were then placed in the folders. It gave him a certain overview. It meant that he could see where the money went. But it didn't make it any easier for him to be parted from it. After dinner, he would sit down in the study and look through his folders with his palm pressed to his forehead. Judging by the sounds he emitted, he might as well have been struggling to hold an angry herd of bulls at bay with nothing but his bare hands. I would be sitting and drawing under the desk, staring at the hairy gap between his trouser legs and socks that was twitching from all the outgoings: life insurance, pension plans, written receipts, lost receipts and *tzorres, tzorres, tzorres.*

But he wasn't a cheapskate. He was just very worried that everything he'd built up was going to fall apart. It could happen at any moment. That was why he was so particular about education. He explained this to me one time when I'd forgotten my history book at school. It was a Friday and we were having a test on Tuesday. When Dad came home and heard about the book, he went crazy. He accelerated down to the school and shook all the locked doors, then went back to the car and drove to a petrol station, found a phone book, then drove to the home of the caretaker, who came back to the school with us and let us in.

Before my bar mitzvah, he drove me to the synagogue every Saturday for almost a year.

He wouldn't allow me to miss a service. But I don't think he did it just for my sake. He enjoyed it too, taking the car in early on a Saturday morning, being able to pick and choose a parking spot, which was only possible at that time of the day in the area around the synagogue.

During the service he would use his index finger to show me where we were in the reading. He underlined the text with it until he could hear that I was keeping up. He jabbed it against the page when he thought I was losing concentration. In between times he mostly sat leaning backwards between Grandad and me, with his prayer book in his lap, twirling the thin white threads of his prayer shawl around his fingers.

On some Saturdays, we stayed behind and took part in the *kiddush* afterwards. Cheese sandwiches were served in the meeting hall, along with coffee and whisky in tiny plastic glasses. Zaddinsky informed everyone about the congregation's financial situation, while old people came up to Dad to tell him about their aches and pains. Worried wives pushed forward reluctant husbands. Embarrassed men discussed potency problems in roundabout ways. Constipated old ladies described their difficulties in great detail: '... all Monday nothing came, nothing at all, even though I drank a pint of water as soon as I got up, then on Tuesday morning I drank a pint and a half, ate a small cauliflower, and I'll tell you what happened...' Dad listened, comforted, explained and conducted examinations. He examined people at the table if it was something innocuous, such as the arm or hand. Otherwise they went in through the swing doors into the kitchen.

Education, Jacob. That was what had helped Dad to advance in record time in the medical hierarchy. He was the youngest doctor in his department. He was chosen to go to the USA and lecture. He had grateful patients all over town who made it possible to finance a large part of the family's expenditure without reference to the tax authorities. If any threatening money clouds appeared on the horizon, such as when friends decided to copy the delightful *goy* habit of going on a skiing holiday, he put in a few extra hours in the study. He wrote down a few extra calculations, while a few extra-large beads of sweat fell on to his notepad, making the figures blurry. Then he picked up the telephone and a few days later a car drew up with its bonnet covered in sports-logo stickers. A bedraggled middle-aged man came in and put ski boots, salopettes, ski gloves and woolly hats on the kitchen table. The man said that that was the least he could do, really the very least.

After Mum and Dad had argued, they usually became friends again in the kitchen in front of the cooker. They cuddled long and hard, while down by their legs Mirra and I joined in the happy reunion. And that's how things went on: he blessed the bread at *shabbat*; he checked I'd done my homework; he relaxed with the day's only cigarette in bed with Mum late at night – until he couldn't resist any longer. Until his arms fell to his sides and the bulls came charging over him.

Grandad left a warm hollow impression behind when he leaned forward. His thin-striped shirt was stretched tight across his broad back, down into his trousers, where his shiny belt with great difficulty managed to hold the shirt in place. For thirty-five years he'd belonged to the burial society – the *chevra* – and never before had recruiting new members been as difficult as now.

The *chevra* performed a very honourable role. Washing the dead and holding vigil over them in the chapel before burial was one of Judaism's most important traditions. Once a year a large party was also organized for all the society's members, which Grandad usually mentioned as a final – and in his eyes unarguable – ace in the hole back in those days when he still discussed the matter with me. Now there was no longer any hope; I wasn't even part of the outer reaches of recruitable young people on whom the society pinned its hopes, and Grandad made no attempt to disguise how unhappy that made him.

Mama Moysowich listened to him with her face full of compassion. They both had similar analyses of what had gone wrong. Almost everybody around our end of the coffee table joined in and repeated the explanations, over and over again, with the same content in slightly different words: young people today don't have the time, they're not interested, they don't understand the significance, no, and they're too busy, there's so much else that interests them, they don't understand its meaning...

Dad had at least agreed to help out on occasion. I remembered that Grandad had raised the matter with him the day after he'd taken his doctoral degree. Dad was leaning back in a garden chair with his arm stretched out behind Mum. He was still a bit shaky after the previous day's celebrations, not to mention the months of effort he'd put in. All spring he'd sat up until late at night and worked behind a tower of books.

Dad smiled kindly and indulgently at Grandad, who with limited success was attempting to chase away the wasps that insisted on returning to his plate. Only as an extra pair of hands, said Grandad, as he tried to convince him. Only when it suits you. They needed all the assistance they could get. Even extra pairs of hands, said Grandad, as he slapped his palm against the outside of the house, are now welcome at the party.

According to Grandad, Grandma's case was an excellent illustration of the staffing problems of the burial society. Her death had been appallingly mismanaged from beginning to end. The fact that as many as five nights had gone by between her passing and the funeral was regrettable. That they hadn't had enough people to hold vigil over her for more than one of them was nothing short of a catastrophe. Grandad pursed his lips. He shook his head, lifted his thus far empty coffee cup, studied something on the inside, then placed it down on the saucer again. It pained him, he said, that members of many years' standing were forced to spend their last night above ground in a mortuary, surrounded by strangers. If you asked the rabbi, he would come and read a *brucha*, which was a slight comfort. However, neither Grandad, Mama Moysowich nor anyone else sitting around the narrow right-hand side of the coffee table thought that this could compare with the treatment that, until quite recently, Gothenburg's deceased Jews would have taken for granted.

The armchair which Mum sat in was broad and equipped with an adjustable neck-rest. As for the feet, there was a retractable support in dark-grey plastic. The armchair's material was deep red and so it deviated a little from the colour scheme in the rest of the living room. From the squat lamps in the corner, via the creamy pink curtains, to the gold-coloured handles shaped as the letters I and D on the veranda doors, there was a consistent and personal theme for which Mum was usually commended.

She was very susceptible to praise. This was particularly the case if it concerned something into which she'd put as much effort as the house. I'd moved out shortly after Mum and Ingemar bought the property. Mirra told me how carefully they decorated each room and almost every time I came to visit I discovered new details: vases on pedestals in the toilet, humorous articles on the window ledges, dolls in long dresses on top of the bookcases.

In the evenings, in front of the TV, Mum came up with new areas which could be furnished. 'A carpet like that possibly, outside Mirra's room… or maybe not, it wouldn't fit, but perhaps a smaller one.' When she didn't think that Ingemar had answered quickly enough, she leaned over towards his armchair and hit him on the fingers. She used to sit with a large bowl of popcorn balanced on her thighs. She liked popcorn, just as she liked all sweets and foods whose name consisted of two short syllables: Tic Tacs, Non Stops, Zig Zags, Sorbits and hot dogs. When I was little and went shopping with her in town, she often thought that we should finish off our outing with a hot dog with mashed potato at Heden Square. As if that wasn't enough of a violation of the *kashrut* laws, she also bought a milk chocolate drink for us to share. We ate on a park bench, huddling close together to protect ourselves from the wind that blew off the sea and swept over the football pitches on the exposed square. In the warmth of the car afterwards she would wipe the ketchup from the corners of my mouth and ask me what we'd eaten. Fishburgers, we'd say in unison, and then we rubbed our thumbs together above the gear stick.

Mum never used the Swedish word for the remote control. She called it 'the remote', in English. She started using that expression during the jet-set years at the beginning of her and Ingemar's marriage, when they both worked a lot and mostly used the house for dropping off bags of duty-free goods and invitation cards. One morning, when they'd returned home from an international conference, Mum announced that they were to stop speaking Swedish at home. 'In order to improve our English, we shall speak only that to each other from now on.' The highpoint of the glamorous era was when they were both pictured in a large celebrity photo in the tabloid magazine *Hänt i veckan*. A hotel that had just opened in the harbour gathered together a large portion of West Sweden's financial, artistic and political elite at its inauguration party. Unaware of what awaited her, Grandma was leafing through the magazine at her hairdresser's. When she saw her daughter and new son-in-law immortalized on the same page as the Mayor of Gothenburg, Göran Johansson, TV interviewer Siewert Öholm and actress Sonya Hedenbratt, she inadvertently scrunched up the page in pure excitement. She called the magazine and ordered five copies, then cut out the photo and stuck it on the fridge. Grandpa in turn took out our old family photograph from the chest of drawers and sellotaped Ingemar's face on top of Dad's.

The broad armchair made a hacking sound when Mum adjusted it to its normal setting. She pointed at a spot in between her shoulders. 'Is anyone going to help me?' Ingemar reluctantly left his place beside Grandpa on the sofa and helped her to remove the orange rubber pillow she'd placed behind her neck. With a mixture of irritated and pleasurable groans, Mum straightened her back, then put her feet in her flip-flops, before disappearing off into the kitchen.

According to Grandpa, Europe was the worst continent in the world.

He was only really comparing it with the USA, and in that trial of strength he found the part of the world he lived in to be inferior in every major respect: films, humour, food.

Within Europe he liked Scandinavia the least. He ranked the Scandinavian countries as follows: 1) Denmark, 2) Norway and 3) Sweden.

He regarded Finland as part of the Soviet Union and therefore not even worthy of consideration.

With regard to Sweden's three largest cities, he could find mitigating factors for Stockholm (large Jewish community) and Malmö (close to Denmark).

He would hold court for entire dinners, in a broad Gothenburg accent, about how awful the city he lived in was: how ugly the city park Slottsskogen was; what a pathetic little cul-de-sac Gothenburg's main street, Avenyn, was from an international perspective; and how foreign tourists jeered at the slim pickings of Liseberg Amusement Park. All the time he would have a large and satisfied smile on his lips.

The only thing he never criticized was IFK Gothenburg Football Club.

You could see the floodlights of the New Ullevi Stadium from the window in Grandpa and Grandma's kitchen. When IFK Gothenburg played, Grandpa was so nervous he couldn't listen to the radio. He sat with his hand in front of his mouth, waiting for the cheering from the ground.

My parents and their friends also used to complain about Gothenburg and Sweden. Sometimes one of them came over, and you knew, just from the way that they pulled out a chair and sank down at the kitchen table, that it was one of those times. That they would soon begin to talk about what a mistake it was that we had ended up here, at the end of the world, with our fate in the hands of a people so up to their ears with their own moral infallibility that they didn't even consider that they needed a god. Everywhere else was better. Every day we stayed was a failure. Since the exodus from Israel it was possible that no Jews had ever been further from home.

I realized that it wasn't as bad as it sounded, but I knew also that it was one of those things that you could never say to people who weren't Jewish.

When Rafael came back from Israel in the summer, he usually started complaining at the airport. The silence in the arrivals hall, the well-organized car park and the lack of traffic on the motorway outside the car window inspired him to long critiques of the country in which he'd grown up.

The first time that Ingemar came along to pick him up, Rafael kept a low profile. He greeted him politely, answered his questions promptly and courteously, while otherwise sitting quietly between Mirra and me in the back seat.

It wasn't until we'd passed some large woods, just before the entrance to the city, that he started up – 'bloody pine trees, damn laws, tasteless food and no traditions, just taxes and drinking and filth and Social Democrats and the arse-licking of the PLO and that politician Gahrton and that journalist Guillou…' – and I heard how Ingemar's breathing in the front seat became more and more strained, until he turned off the road and, with clenched jaws, declared that he would *not* tolerate that type of discussion in his car.

There had been similar arguments down the years. They often started between Rafael and Ingemar, but after a few minutes everyone was involved. The arguments never really stopped; they just had small intervals during which everyone could catch their breath and bathe their wounds before gathering strength for the next round. A few times Mirra tried to get everyone to sit down together in the living room and clear the air.

Ingemar and Mum would sit on one side of the coffee table, while Rafael, Mirra and I sat on the other, all accompanied by glowering looks and folded arms. Sometimes a girlfriend or boyfriend was there too. If Papa Moysowich came by, he usually sat down and observed the showdown from a chair at the dining table. The sessions could last for an hour or so, invariably resulting in new arguments, between Mum and Ingemar, between us siblings, until someone finally dared to mention Dad, whereupon Mum would storm up to the bedroom, tears pouring down her cheeks, beating her hands against her ears and with her slightly abrasive voice cranked up to maximum volume: 'Just keep going, everything is my fault, I'm the worst mother in the world. Let's all join in – there goes the worst mother in the world, there goes the worst mother in the world.'

On the morning of Yom Kippur, the second of the autumn's main holidays, Mirra and I sat in our best clothes at the breakfast table. I didn't eat the bread or the biscuits that had been placed on the table, nor did I drink the tea. It was my first Yom Kippur since my bar mitzvah. For the first time, I was included in the edict to fast for the whole day.

The folds at the back of Mum's white dressing gown were beating like bat's wings every time she stood up. She got her packet of cigarettes, adjusted Mirra's hair and made some more coffee when she noticed she'd already emptied her cup. Normally she would take just the odd gulp during breakfast, before carrying the cup around with her throughout the house. It came with her to the kitchen sink, to the basin in front of the bathroom mirror and was finally abandoned on the chest of drawers in the bedroom, with a cold light-brown splash at its bottom and a large pink lipstick smudge at the rim.

Mirra and I went out into the hall a few minutes after Papa Moysowich had called and said that he was on his way. I had my hand on the lock of the outside door, when Mum asked one last time if we really weren't disappointed that she wasn't coming with us. We knew which answer she wanted and competed to deliver it in the most emphatic manner possible. 'Are you sure?' she shouted from the kitchen. I said yes. I told her that the rabbi had even said that there were people in the congregation who thought it would be best if she didn't come.

For a brief moment things went quiet in the kitchen. Then I heard Mum angrily begin to clear the table, then set about the kitchen cupboards. Ingemar raised a few careful objections to the decision she was about to take. Less than half an hour later,

Mum skidded his Volvo into a vacant space next to the sports shop at the back of the synagogue.

Mirra and I half-ran behind her. Her heels clattered against the ground. She pulled open the brown doors, dragged Mirra with her up the stairs to the women's balcony on the right-hand side, before clambering over the cluster of legs with her black coat under her arm.

Down below among the men, the Nightingale turned around and hissed, with his finger in front of his large blue lips. The rabbi cleared his throat, some people stamped on the floor, but the murmuring only increased and it didn't stop until Zaddinsky clapped his hands and thundered, '*Schweig!*'

Dad was wearing his black suit. He had on a dark tie with a gold pin.

We were standing near the middle of the left-hand row of pews. Grandad had the seat next to the aisle. Dad had the one next to him. Two small rectangular plates with their names in white lettering against a grey background were attached to the book-rest in front of us.

Dad's large high holidays prayer book lay open, with its spine resting against the brown wood. One page fluttered in the air, as if it couldn't make up its mind in which direction to go.

In the box which belonged to Dad's seat, we each had our own blue satin bag with a prayer shawl – *tallit* – and phylacteries – *tefillin*. A dirty woollen mitten had also ended up there, together with a New Year's greeting Mirra had made during her Hebrew lessons.

Dad stood with his arms close to his body, chewing his thumbnail. I put on my *tallit* myself, leaned against the pew and rested my head on my hands.

The hours passed slowly.

Torah scrolls were removed from the ark and everybody had to stand up. Old men were called up to read. The cantor marked the place to read by running a metal pointer across the scripture. The old men finished reading and the Torah scrolls were carried round. Then you had to sit for twenty minutes before it all started again.

I counted the Stars of David in the carpet on the underside of the balcony. After that I went out for a short while to drink some water. When I came back, I noticed that the *schtunken* was well under way.

The *schtunken* was what arose when hundreds of fasting people spent an entire day in the same hall. It smelled like a mixture of acetone and old rubbish. It grew worse with every hour that passed. It made late arrivals turn on their heels and leave. It made pregnant women stagger towards the exit with their hands across their mouths. It came seeping from the oral cavities of old people, pushed through the remnants of food between their teeth, taking with it the smell of expectation among the gossips on the back row, along with the stale exhaled breath from the loose-skinned prefects who shushed them. It sucked up the contents of babies' heavy nappies and the snotty-nosed whinings of their older siblings. It mixed with the parts that were difficult to wash in the rabbi's beard and rose, rose, rose all twenty-six feet to the ceiling, where it gathered force, turned and dived back down over balconies and pews.

My feet were cold. Jonathan Friedkin walked past our seats and asked if I wanted to come with him to the child-minding area in the meeting hall. I said no.

The blood collected at my fingertip, making it red, purple, then blue. I pulled the thread harder round the highest of my index finger's three horizontal lines and waited for the throbbing, until I let go and saw the colour disappear along with the blood. It continued to throb for a while afterwards, getting weaker and weaker, until all that was left was a tickling buzz at the very top of my finger.

If I held my hand at a right angle, the veins on the back became almost as broad as Dad's. On my left hand they looked like a Y, with long, sinewy branches up towards my fingers. Those were the type of hands I wanted. Hands you could use to beat the rhythm against your knees; hands you could use to pat the back of someone who'd done something well. A proper backslap and a firm handshake: *Shkoyach*, my friend, really *shkoyach*.

At my bar mitzvah, people left their seats to come forward and congratulate me at the very same moment that I'd finished reading my portion of the Torah. Peanuts rained down on my head from the balcony and I received solid thumps on my back from some men, hearty grasps of the shoulder from others, ostentatious hugs from the women, cold hands and damp kisses from the old people.

Only Moshe Dayan was grumpy that time. He didn't like the tradition of throwing peanuts over the young people having their bar and bat mitzvahs. He was the one who had to clean up the synagogue afterwards, rub away the grease stains from the red carpet, dig away the grains of salt from the metal rods which fastened the stair carpet leading up to the ark and sweep away the trails of crushed peanuts that had collected on each and every one of the three steps. He wasn't alone in cleaning the synagogue, but it was he who took the job most seriously. It was he who took greatest responsibility for its appearance and who saw every unnecessary soiling of its interior as a personal insult. 'The lollipops,' he used to say when he turned around on his way out to the courtyard and, for mainly masochistic reasons, witnessed the destruction once more. 'Why couldn't we just have continued with the lollipops?'

For several years, the girls had thrown down chocolate lollipops from the balcony in order to mark the ceremony. Moshe Dayan praised the lollipops retrospectively, but the truth was that he hadn't been happy with them either. Even lollipops resulted in rubbish – paper everywhere, lollipop sticks too, and always some kid who just ate half of his and dropped the rest on the carpet. It usually remained lying there, trodden underfoot and stuck to the floor. In addition, many elderly visitors were terrified at the thought of being hit by one of the lollipops. 'They get heavy when they fall from such a height,' Dayan had said back in the days when it was the chocolate lollipops he was fighting against. 'What was wrong with those tiny pastel sweets?'

It was Rabbi Weizmann who'd taken the decision about the peanuts. He'd suggested a salt-free variety when Dayan complained. No salt, no grease stains, no mocking fragments playing hide-and-seek under the metal rods on the stairs. The caretaker was not prepared to go that far, however. Without salt, how will they taste? Take away the salt from peanuts and what do you have left? A knotty lump of wood. Dry. Tasteless. It wasn't a worthy way to welcome a Jewish child on the day he or she entered adulthood; he would rather take upon himself the drudgery, but – and this the rabbi should be quite clear about – he wouldn't do it with joy.

Every time we changed rabbi there was a re-evaluation of what produce would be allowed on the premises. A list of permitted items was sent by the Chief Rabbi in Stockholm once a year. It was supposed to apply uniformly to all Sweden's congregations, but our rabbis never paid any attention to it. Every new rabbi had his own interpretation of the *kashrut* laws and went systematically through everything: the cheese in the fridge up in the hall's kitchen; the coffee; the dried milk powder; the juice concentrate; the *kiddush* wine; Zaddinsky's sugar-free digestive biscuits and Zelda's meat-flavoured doggy treats. Each rabbi then wrote new laws.

Sweets were given an especially intensive examination. They were regarded as extra special since they belonged to young people's field of interest. We were the growing generation, the future. It was of extreme importance that we didn't consume anything that might set us on the wrong path. The chocolate lollipops were always in the danger zone, accepted by one rabbi, forbidden by the next. The same went for the tiny pastel sweets. These were generally accepted by European rabbis and blacklisted by American ones.

No one could adequately explain why our congregation changed rabbi so often. The explanations that were proposed – poor climate, small congregation, remote country – were not convincing. Other Scandinavian congregations had similar conditions yet still managed to keep their rabbis. In Copenhagen they'd had the same man for fifteen years.

There was a degree of uncertainty about how many we'd got through during the same period. It depended on how you counted. For instance, should you only include those who'd really been rabbis, or even those who'd claimed to be one? Should you count those whom the congregation's Board of Trustees had got on well with, who'd signed a contract, but then never turned up? And what about those who'd been present – introduced under the headline 'AT LAST' in a wide shot on the front page of the congregation's newsletter? Those pictured with a big smile, with their shoulders covered by Zaddinsky's outstretched arm, but who'd disappeared without trace before the next issue of the newsletter had gone to print – should they be counted?

I recalled a Belgian with a red beard, a slightly absent-minded Israeli, one who'd been in a Soviet labour camp and had bad breath and one who spoke only German and used to throw me up in the air in the entrance hall. My parents used to talk about Rosen. He'd come to the congregation one spring evening some time in the mid-1970s. Zaddinsky had been the last one left in the building, sitting in the beige sunken armchair in his office, sticking address labels on payment reminder notices, when the entry phone's insistent buzzer had cut through the premises. On the black and white monitor in the reception he saw a young man with a tight jacket and bushy hair. The stranger had a military bag in one hand and with the other he held up a rabbinical identity card towards the security camera.

He'd come by boat, said he was from Boston, but spoke English with a slight Spanish accent. During the following months he transformed the synagogue's otherwise peaceful activities into wild, fiery exhibitions. He extended the Friday service to over three hours. He walked around between the pews, called down women from the balcony, interrupted prayers to ask questions, demanded answers and didn't stop until he believed he could feel God's presence in the room.

Then, one day, he too was gone. No one had any idea of where he'd disappeared to. No congregation in Boston knew anyone of his name. The rabbinical seminary that had issued his diploma confirmed that he'd been a student, but they didn't know of any family or any close friends. The only clue that came to light was that Katzman's cousin had seen someone who resembled him lead a group of tourists through an alleyway somewhere in India. The alleyway was narrow and full of people, so she hadn't had a chance to get up close in order to see properly.

Certain people claimed that there was a curse upon us. Once upon a time we had been like other congregations, with rabbis who stayed until they got too ancient, too ill or just plain died.

A very long time ago, before the war even, we'd had an old man who refused to resign, even though he was over ninety years old. He was so weak that two men had to help him walk up on to the *bima*. His voice was so faint that only those who stood closest could hear him. Despite this, he still insisted on conducting every service. Not even the fact that, with increasing frequency, he dropped a Torah scroll when he lifted it out of the ark made him change his mind. This was even though the punishment for such a transgression is a total of forty days' fasting. Forty days which, since it is too much to ask of one individual, have to be shared between those who were present at the time the scroll fell.

The old rabbi grew more frail and more stubborn every year he survived. After one particularly harsh winter, there wasn't much more left of him than a transparent skeleton. Every time he approached the ark to grasp a scroll, the entire congregation held its breath. After a while, people started to clap their hands. Nothing helped. He dropped the scrolls every time. At the major festivals and at the minor ones, on *shabbat* and on weekdays, at the morning services, at the afternoon ones, as well as on Sundays, when they were only brought out to be dusted off. He dropped them on the synagogue's wooden floorboards and on the red carpet, he dropped them on the steps down from the *bima*, and he dropped one right down on top of the others in the ark, which caused a chain reaction whereby all the scrolls fell out, rolled down and crash-landed in front of the first pew.

The Board of Trustees at the time worked out that, even if all the accumulated days up to that point were divided among all the adult members of the congregation, as well as those boys who were to have their bar mitzvahs within one year, they would still have to fast for nearly a month each. They didn't think that there was any point in antagonizing the members by demanding such huge sacrifices, when they would soon only

84

have to demand new ones. They decided to draw a line under what had happened and stop counting.

Only when we had redeemed that crime would the curse be lifted.

Dad folded up his *tallit*, then placed it in the box. He borrowed a lighter from a man in the pew in front of us. The man had the beginnings of a beard growing underneath his chin.

I pushed my hands against the sides of my body and looked down at the floor. When I wiggled my feet from side to side, it looked as though the tassels on my loafers were dancing with each other. I'd noticed that for the first time when I was standing with Sanna Grien at my bar mitzvah party. Her family had been among the first to arrive. After I'd opened their presents, we'd stood next to each other, with our backs to the table with the presents on it. We didn't say much, just stood there in all our finery, looking around the room at the elegantly laid tables. I started to shake the tassels on my shoes and gave them pretend voices. Sanna laughed so much that she got hiccups, which made her laugh even more. She hadn't even stopped when Grandad, Mame and Aunt Irene arrived shortly afterwards. Mame had handed over their present, with her voice and hands quivering with solemnity. I had to pretend that I was curious about what was inside the wrapping paper, even though Mame had told me several months earlier. 'Now, I don't want you to tell your mother and father,' she'd said. 'But for your bar mitzvah, Jacob, I want to give you something important. A memory. Not a new jumper. Not a hundred-kronor note in an envelope. I'm going to give you –' her eyes had edged sideways to check that no one was eavesdropping – 'a *kiddush* cup, which you can use your whole life. Do you want to see it now?'

My stomach rumbled softly. My shins hurt and the small of my back was sore.

The surface of the pew was covered with several layers of

brown paint, a creamy shade, like chocolate pudding. It was smooth when you rested your cheek against it. I counted how long I could keep my mouth open without starting to drool: 1, 2, 3. I counted the seconds in my head: 34, 35, 36. I closed my eyes: 71, 72, 73. Yom Kippur, 1973. The air-raid siren had gone off at two o'clock in the afternoon. Shortly afterwards the information had reached the news agencies. The rabbi cut short the service, whereupon everybody rushed to the congregation building. The long shirt collars and heavy sideburns made it extra crowded in Zaddinsky's office. I was in Mum's womb at the time. Rafael looked like Mowgli. Dad didn't have a moustache.

I wish I'd been there on that occasion. The entire congregation gathered in front of a crackly radio, while a few people hurried away to call relatives in Israel and children in warm sweaters played on the floor. I could have been one of them. Dad could have called Rafael and me to his side, sat us on his knee, then explained what had happened: about the shocking attacks from the north and the south, about our troops standing back to back, about the headquarters in Jerusalem where our sharpest minds and our bravest hearts were now doing everything they could to maybe, just maybe, turn the impossible situation around.

... 89, 90, 91. A darkened room: 102, 103, 104. Nervous politicians: 117, 118, 119. Terrible news from the front. Golda lit cigarette after cigarette and called her ministers idiots. They hadn't been able to detect the smell of war in the air and now they'd failed to get planes quickly enough from the USA. The country was only hours from destruction, unless something extraordinary happened. Golda saw the prospect of a bloodbath ahead. Perhaps our enemies would show greater mercy if we surrendered immediately. Yes, she decided, that's how it would have to be. She was standing with the phone in her hand when I appeared in the room. 'Wait,' I shouted. A colonel laughed at me. Golda said, 'Quiet, let the boy speak.' Simultaneously, the map on the wall behind us changed to black and white pictures of pioneers fighting their way across hostile desert terrain; trainloads of deportees from the war swept past, while Nazis with rifles pushed prisoners in front of them. There was Ben-Gurion at the museum in Tel Aviv, there were the soldiers by the Wailing Wall, there were Grandad and Mame on holiday in Natanya, there were light-skinned, dark-skinned, European and Far Eastern children all together at a playschool. They were all lined up in rows and singing 'Hatikvah'.

I jerked up my head, then wiped my face with the back of my hand. A saliva pool the size of a large coin had formed on the book-rest below my mouth. My heart beat quickly. I looked straight ahead over the rows of pews, before trying to strike a pose so self-assured and casual that it would compensate for how I had just been day-dreaming. It wasn't possible. I pushed my hands deep into my pockets and made my way out down the aisle.

I looked in at the reception, then continued on towards the entrance hall outside Zaddinsky's office. I went into the toilets and saw that all the cubicles were empty.

Mirra was playing a game of 'It' with her friends in the stairwell. When I asked her if she'd seen Dad, she shook her head.

I walked up the stairs with my hand on the black plastic banister. The doors to the meeting hall were locked. No one was sitting in the wooden armchairs outside.

In one of the classroom on the third floor, several desks had been put together to form two rows, lined up on either side of the teacher's desk. Little children were making bead mosaics, others were filling in crossword pages with Hebrew and English text. On a chair next to the blackboard there was a stack of the 1977 summer edition of the cartoon magazine *Illustrerade klassiker*.

The edition dealt with the exodus from Egypt, and the congregation had bought up about a hundred copies. They were to be found lying about discarded under the sofa down in the bar, or in nooks and crannies behind the stage in the meeting hall. They were also the only illustrated magazines that could be borrowed from the library further down the corridor. When I was younger, I'd only been able to read the first half. Everything had been fine while Moses was a child and living as a prince. But later, when he'd found out who he really was, had killed a brutal overseer, hidden in the desert, spoken to God and returned to liberate his people, I'd had to stop. In the magazine Pharaoh was completely bald, with fierce eyes that grew more cruel the angrier he became with the stubborn Israelites. I knew

89

that I wouldn't be able to sleep if I looked at him too much. Sometimes I'd sat down with the magazine in front of me, opened it at a page near the end and stared right into Pharaoh's horrible eyes, before quickly closing it again.

A strong smell of cooked food from the Chinese restaurant swept in through the open window. Jonathan Friedkin was sitting with Sanna Grien and Alexandra in the far corner of the room. He waved me over. He had a deck of cards in his hand. On the table was a pad of writing paper, along with a half-eaten sandwich. A plastic cup that had contained orange juice lay on its side nearby. A few drops were still left, in the ridges on the side and in the ring at the bottom.

Jonathan divided the deck into two halves, then pushed the edges against each other. Sanna scrawled a large cross through the three columns she'd drawn on the square-patterned paper in front of her. She then put a line across the middle of the page, before making four new columns underneath. Using capital letters, she wrote our names at the top of the columns.

Alexandra won the first round. We were halfway through the second when voices could be heard from the courtyard below. Everyone in the room ran over to the window and looked at the drama that was being enacted three storeys below. We saw a guard come rushing from the rear of the building. From the synagogue came women without their coats. Men ran out with one hand holding their *kippa* on their head. In front of the entrance to the congregation building they formed a circle in the midst of which stood my father, gripping my mother's arms. Someone was trying to get him to break his hold.

I had grabbed one of the long white curtains and peered out through a gap.

At my bar mitzvah party, when almost everyone had gone home, my mother and father went out on to the dance floor. They glided around, holding each other close, underneath the hall's chandelier. I stood by the stereo, thinking that they'd just been stressed before the party; that that was why they'd argued so much recently. The following morning, I sat with my hands over my ears on the floor of my room. When I finally opened the door, I saw wrapping paper lying ripped to shreds, while other paper was scrunched up all over the hall's wall to wall carpet. I found a book under the sofa and a camera by the toilet door. The *kiddish* cup had fallen down the stairs to the floor below.

It was a few days later that Dad's colleague called. He said that Dad was exhausted from too much work and would be staying at his house in the country over the weekend. When Dad returned, late on Sunday evening, his colleague was with him. He held Dad up when he staggered over the threshold into the kitchen. He told Dad that they had arrived, then suggested he say something to us. Dad was shaking as though he had a fever.

Down in the courtyard, two men helped to disperse the crowd. I pulled some leaves off a dark-green plant on the window ledge. Behind my back, I heard Alexandra say she wanted to play another round.

Mirra's warm little hand came and grasped mine. I dried her cheeks, then spun her into the curtain, hard, so that she looked like a small Russian doll, then out quickly again. She started to laugh and wanted me to do it again.

My Grandad looked like an ape. His head sat low between high-pulled-up shoulders, and when he scratched his ear he used the arm on the other side. Just like an ape. When he got up from his armchair in the evenings, he sounded like an ape. He grunted as he walked to the bathroom and turned on the taps by the washbasin. His hands weren't really suited for the delicate manoeuvring that was needed in there. He held his toothbrush as though it were a ski pole and squeezed the toothpaste tube far too hard. When he was finished with his teeth, he had to wipe away several inches of long white toothpaste tendrils from the basin using toilet paper.

Grandad wasn't in the least surprised when I told him that I associated him more with apes than with normal people. Instead he reacted as though I was on the trail of something important. Perhaps he was rather impressed that I had realized his true nature at such a young age.

Mame and he had apes everywhere in their flat. There was a reddish-brown porcelain gorilla on a window ledge and a book with chimpanzees on the cover in the bookshelf. In the bedroom was a drawing I had done of King Louie from the Disney film *The Jungle Book*. The drawing remained pinned up on the bedroom wall for a long time.

The book about chimpanzees was one of fourteen volumes in a series with brown spines that dealt with the animal kingdom by continent. When we arrived at their flat I would get a chair from the kitchen, climb up, take down *Africa 4*, then give it to Grandad. In the middle there was a photo identical to the one on the cover. A young ape was captured in profile, suspended between two branches, his mouth shaped as though he was whistling. Grandad flipped quickly between the inside and the outside, tricking me into believing that the ape was swinging from one place to the other. When we had done that a few times, he started flipping between the inside front and inside back covers, which both showed two black and white apes with their fur smoothed down in a centre parting over the top of their head.

Grandad had a frayed brown dressing gown that reached down to his knees. When Mirra and I spent the night, I used to wake up hearing him shuffling to the toilet.

We made breakfast together when he was finished. I set the table, while Grandad cut large slices of bread. There were poppy seeds and crumbs on the chopping board. The cheese lay under a plastic cover. I ate sandwiches with Grandad. Then, when Mirra and Mame joined us at the table, I ate cornflakes. They'd bought the cereal for our sakes and let us have as much sugar as we liked. Afterwards I lay on the kitchen floor with a heap of old *Göteborgs Tidningen* newspapers. I read the sports pages and the cartoons. 'Look,' I heard Grandad and Mame say to each other, 'just like Josef when he was small.'

Grandad would call me to his side and lift me up on to his knees. His smile was broad in anticipation. Jacob, he'd say. Who's on top of the league in… he put a finger on his chin… Holland?

That was easy. Ajax.

He looked at Mame. They laughed. Look at what the boy knows. Fantastic.

Italy? Juventus.

England? Liverpool.

Spain? Real Madrid.

Poland? Real Warszawa.

I could say anything. They had no idea.

Grandad had played handball when he was young. He had three younger siblings. A few months before Hitler's troops marched into Poland, Grandad was contacted by an organization that, for a low fee, helped Jews to get to *kibbutzim* in Palestine. He set aside part of the wages he earned as a tailor's apprentice and applied for himself and his siblings. Their parents were to join them shortly afterwards, or so they planned.

When the siblings were told to disembark after several days' journey, they noticed that their destination wasn't Jerusalem, Haifa, or any other of the mythical places Grandad had fantasized about as he leaned his face against the porthole during their trip.

It was called Silkeborg.

On a small farm in the Danish countryside, a group of East European Jews were to be prepared for the physical work that would be demanded of them in the building of a Jewish state. Four months of training was what was needed, the organizers promised. They remained there for three years.

When the Germans invaded Denmark, their accommodation was transformed into a sealed-up hiding place. Grandad and his siblings survived on handouts from a farmer on an adjacent farm. One morning, when the farmer had left his food basket, he told Grandad to come with him. Later that evening, Grandad returned with a note on which someone had written a date and a time. For two days, they waited inside a fishing boat in the harbour. The five siblings lay packed tightly together underneath a tarpaulin. They heard German voices conversing on the quay.

It was snowing in Gothenburg when they arrived. At the congregation building Grandad was introduced to a man who looked him over, then said he had room for all the siblings in his flat. The man lived in a one-bedroom apartment in the district of Majorna. He had three daughters, one of whom, at the age of twenty-six, was still unmarried. Grandad and Mame's marriage was held three weeks after they'd seen each other for the first time.

Grandad's siblings emigrated to Israel after the war. Every other summer, Mame and Grandad went and visited. Mame very much wanted to go somewhere else. She'd painted a lot of pictures with Parisian themes, even though she'd never been there. They lay rolled up in rubber bands at the top of the cupboard in the hallway. Mame needed a chair to reach them. She placed ashtrays and cups on the corners to keep the paintings flat. There were women in short skirts. Women with hats at a jaunty angle. Women dressed for spring weather, walking off in different directions, with the outline of the Eiffel Tower behind them.

But it didn't have to be Paris. Anywhere in southern Europe was fine. Yugoslavia, Italy, Portugal or Spain. In Spain they had something called *gazpacho*, an ice-cold red soup she'd tasted on one occasion. And they'd had loads of Jews there once upon a time. You could still tell: when Mame heard Spanish songs on the radio, she recognized Jewish rhythms and melodies. 'It's in the blood, *kindlach*. They speak right to the heart. All my life I've dreamed of Spain,' she said. Sometimes Grandad would nod in approval. Then they ended up going to Israel anyway.

Mirra and I used to go with Dad to drop them off at Landvetter Airport. Mame sat between us in the back seat. Grandad sat in the front with their passports in his hand. When they'd checked in, they gave us their coats and took the escalators up. Dad bought three ice creams in the café underneath the giant globe.

Four weeks later, they came back with a T-shirt each for Mirra and me and a large bag of Israeli biscuits, along with a bottle of spirits that Grandad placed on the top shelf above the desk and never opened.

He didn't actively avoid alcohol; it's just that he wasn't interested in it. He hadn't had to tell me – it was easy to work out from his way of merely dutifully sipping the *shabbat* evening *kiddush* wine – but he had told me anyway. We sat on their balcony, the only time we ever sat there. He was serious and focused. He spoke more slowly and clearly than usual, but his ability to handle Swedish colloquial phrases still hadn't improved.

'I've never been teetotal, you know,' he said, before looking at me for a long time. 'Swedes love to go teetotal. Many of my competitors disappeared because they went teetotal so often. I hope that you'll never be teetotal, Jacob. Can you promise me that?'

During the approximately forty minutes that we spent on the balcony, Mame didn't come out to us once. It was a few years after everything had happened and it's possible that they'd planned that Grandad was to talk to me about the difficult issues. But then he lost his courage and the seriousness emerged instead as warnings about the dangers of drinking. Most of what he said didn't even amount to that. It was more of a loud inner monologue in which he tried to come to an agreement with himself about what the Swedish licensing laws were like in the 1960s. I looked down the street, trying to imagine what it must have been like to lean over the edge of the balcony and chat to some friends who'd come by to talk about a newly released Beatles single. I only became properly attentive when Grandad told me that he'd once caught Dad red-handed in front of the shelf with the spirits on it. Dad had been fourteen or fifteen. He'd been standing on the desk, with two miniature bottles between his feet and his right hand about to grasp a bottle of liqueur, when Grandad had entered the room. Grandad had shouted so loudly that Dad almost fell over. Then he'd begun to cry, said Grandad, and folded his arms.

With that, the window of opportunity was closed. I asked a few careful questions, made a few subtle hints, but everything returned to normal. Nothing I did could open that window again.

Gunshots were fired in a refugee camp, four settlers opened fire on a crowd of people. One seventeen-year-old girl was dead, two fourteen-year-olds were injured. There was a bomb in a rubbish bin, and a guerrilla soldier in a parachute. Six were dead. Seven were injured. There were provocative statements from Shamir, threatening comments by Arafat, and on a cold, rainy Friday afternoon, Dad came round to the house to spend the weekend with us.

I didn't hear the front door open. I was at home on my own, the stereo was on, playing loudly, and I had spent the whole of the previous half-hour with my upper body deep inside Ingemar's drinks cabinet. The result of my efforts was a Coke bottle full of a pale urine-coloured alcohol mixture. I had just sealed the bottle with a green plastic cap when Dad stepped into the hall.

I pushed the bottle behind a cushion on the sofa before going to embrace him. The smell of aftershave on his neck had mixed with petrol and outdoor cold. He noticed that I'd had a haircut and said that it looked good. He had a plastic bag with him from the shop with all the things Mirra and I had told him to buy. Potatoes, thin frying steak, tomatoes, bread in a brown paper bag, a large bar of chocolate and a packet of salt liquorice laces.

We put the meat in the fridge and Dad told me about the flat he'd managed to get. It was in the district of Masthugget, near the square. You could see the sea from the balcony. He said he'd buy a bunk bed for the room that Mirra and I were to have. His clothes were in a red and white sports bag that he put on the sofa bed in the study. I asked if he'd brought his blue and white striped shirt with him, and if so, if I could borrow it. He asked what I was planning to do. I answered that I was going to go to a disco with some girls from school, which was true, and that Jonathan was coming too, which was a lie.

He pulled open the zip, then lifted his clothes out on to the sofa. The bag collapsed in on itself when it was emptied, while the round symbol on its side became as low and broad as a skateboard.

Dad seemed slightly troubled by the fact that I wasn't going to be home that evening. But he was also curious. He wanted to know more about these girls. While he brought out his shirt, he asked me who they were, if I thought any of them were pretty and if any of them seemed to have a crush on me.

I went upstairs and took a shower. The door was open and when I was drying myself, I saw that Dad had picked up the clothes that I'd thrown down and put them on the sofa. He was walking about slowly in the hall outside, looking around. He didn't say anything about the lighter section on the wallpaper where the oval frame with the wedding photo had been. Nor did he mention the dark-violet dressing gown that hung next to Mum's on the inside of the bathroom door.

Whenever we met, he used to want to hear about everything that was happening at home. Before he dropped me off, he frequently drove around in the car for a while longer. He questioned me about what everyday life with Ingemar was like, whether he usually came in and said goodnight to us in the evenings, and if he comforted Mirra when she was upset. Between the questions he sat in silence for long periods, stroking the two middle fingers of his left hand back and forth across his moustache. I made a special effort to tell him edited versions of the truth, but he saw through me easily. After a while he would begin to swear and get heated, so I'd say, 'Well, don't ask me, then,' and he'd say, 'I know, I know.'

Sometimes, when we got annoyed with each other, I said things that I regretted later, like it was better that they were divorced than that they argued, or that Mum seemed to be much happier now. He used to dismiss that at first, saying, 'That's what she says, I can just hear her saying that,' but then, when I'd continue on in the same manner, he got angry and raised his voice. After that, he usually became quiet and pursed his lips. Once he had to swing the car over into a parking space at the side of the road. He sat bent forward, holding the steering wheel in a tight grip. His upper body trembled in waves. I patted him on the neck and back, saying sorry, but he shook his head and said that it was he who should apologize.

I buttoned my shirt in front of the mirror. I lowered the volume on the cassette recorder outside the bathroom in order to be able to hear Dad's footsteps downstairs. When I came downstairs, he was standing in front of a painting in the living room. It was a dark-red picture of two figures with pale faces who were hovering over a city. I had always thought it was a good picture. I knew the motif was a Jewish one, but not in what way. It didn't contain any famous symbols; there were no Hebrew characters, or any other of the usual features. Dad's gaze was directed at the white portion at the bottom of the painting, where some dates were displayed and the artist's name was written with a sophisticated calligraphy that I had never been able to decipher.

I sat on the sofa, sneaking my hand carefully behind its back in order to push down the bottle. Dad asked if there was anything in particular I would like to do that weekend. He'd promised Mirra that we would go into town and visit the shops on one of the days. On Saturday night, we were to have dinner with Bernie and Teresza. When he caught sight of the new glass table between the sofas he was impressed. He raised his eyebrows, then felt the thin pane between his thumb and his index finger on either side. An old wooden table had stood there previously, which he'd collected after he'd moved into his flat. Ingemar and I had carried it out. We had placed it in the car park, together with a few bags of books and four dining chairs, as well as two boxes of plates and glasses which had been labelled with yellow stickers. Ingemar helped Dad to load the things when he and Bernie had arrived with the removal van. They small-talked all the while. It sounded as if they were having quite a nice time, as though both of them were really trying not to cause the other any inconvenience.

'Dad, this is for you.'

Mirra came in from the hall with her shoes and her jacket on. Her rucksack was hanging down a bit over her left upper arm. She tried to take off the rucksack and open it at the same time. Dad helped her pull out a collage of magazine cuttings she'd made at school. When Mirra had taken off her jacket, she wanted Dad to come up with her to her room. I took the opportunity to get the bottle from the sofa and went outside to put it in the mailbox.

After a while, Dad came down to the kitchen with a pile of drawings and an oven glove which he put next to the radio. Mirra opened the fridge. She emptied the bag with the potatoes in the sink, took out the two sharpest knives and the large chopping board from the drawer, putting everything on the kitchen table. She and Dad cut the potatoes into small pieces, which they put on an oven tray, before seasoning them with paprika. Mirra tasted one of the raw potato pieces, then mimicked a grumpy dance teacher she had. As she helped me set the table, she imitated the teacher's walk, with her bottom stuck out and her face in a strained expression. Dad and I laughed at her, which made her laugh even more. She wanted to stand beside Dad, watching him while he fried the meat, and she didn't even get upset when some hot drops of olive oil spattered up from the frying pan and burned her.

I went and got the *kippot* and the prayer book: the *siddur*. Mirra and I blessed the candles together; Dad blessed the wine and then the bread, pulling off small pieces and pressing them against the holes in the salt cellar before passing them round. He even made the special blessings over Mirra and me, which he had often done when we were younger. He stood between us and recited, with his hand first on her head, then on mine.

We ate until there was nothing left of the potatoes, the meat or the salad with the tomatoes and red onions. I quickly wiped up the last remnants of sauce with the bread, then said that I had to hurry. Mirra didn't know that I was going out and she looked in confusion first at me, then at Dad. I ran up to the bathroom, brushed my teeth and put on some extra aftershave. When I came downstairs again, Mirra asked what we should do with the sweets. She felt sorry for me because I wasn't going to have any and said that we should eat them at once, before I went out. I said that wasn't necessary, but she insisted. I said that I didn't care about sweets and she got angry, shouting that I couldn't always decide everything. It was only when Dad suggested that they could save some for me that she calmed down, but when I shut the door, she still had that strained expression on her face that she got when something worried her.

The rain beat down against the mailbox. Almost the whole bottle fitted inside my jacket's inner pocket. I pulled the zip all the way up to my throat. Through the windows I saw the *shabbat* candles flickering on the kitchen table. The door of the dishwasher was fully open and the upper tray had been pulled out. Dad had lifted Mirra up on to the sink, saying something that had made her laugh again.

I was back before eleven o'clock. Dad's jumper had fallen down from a chair in the hall. The lights in the kitchen as well as in the living room were on. Music was coming from the stereo. The TV was on too but no one was sitting in front of it. In the morning, Mirra woke me up and pulled me over to the stairs. We pressed our faces to the wooden slats, peering into the kitchen, where Dad sat shakily holding the telephone receiver.

Half an hour later, Grandad came by and picked him up. When they'd driven off, I dialled the number on the note that Mum had put on the fridge.

When there were twenty minutes left of the lesson, Miss Judith said that it was my turn to give a talk. She claimed that I was supposed to have prepared one about the 1982 Lebanon War. There was something vaguely familiar about this information which made it difficult for me to protest.

I walked up to the blackboard. The room was completely silent while I rustled through my papers. Lebanon '82. It hadn't been much of a war, I knew that much. Apart from that, everything was a blank. The information was there really, somewhere in the back of my head, but other images were in the way. Israel went into Lebanon in the summer of 1982, but why, and what happened after that? Had we even won? I had no idea any more.

All I could see in front of me was a radio, which had been moved from the kitchen and was now on the veranda at the Moysowichs' country cottage. The antenna had been fully extended, while the various dads were fiddling with the round tuning dial. There was pink outdoor furniture on the veranda, along with a loose plank around which you had to be careful. An impressive Hungarian chocolate cake stood on a rickety table in the shade.

Once an hour the radio had been turned on, while worried remarks were exchanged across the veranda. Sanna Grien dressed up Mirra in old clothes she found in a chest. Jonathan was wearing an Argentinian football top. Zelda was a puppy and Rafael and I gave her the leftovers of our cake. She threw up in the flowerbed later on.

A rectangular lawn spread out beneath the veranda. Two birch trees formed a natural goal at one end, while at the other someone had hammered in two thin wooden poles.

In order to reach the beach, you had to walk for about ten minutes through some woods. Dad built a sandcastle for me once. I had a red toy car with me and he made a street around the castle. Then he created an entire community of buildings, bridges, towers and roads. I didn't want to drive the car on it, so instead I crawled slowly around the town and imagined the small beings who lived there. Before I'd even managed to crawl round an entire circuit, Mirra ran right across it all. She laughed jeeringly and I chased her out into the water to get my revenge. Dad got there ahead of us. He grabbed hold of us both, threw us in the air and caught us just before we hit the water.

Mum came running out to us with her hands in the air. She didn't really like swimming. She dipped her hands in now and then, splashing some water across each shoulder, but this time she dived right in. Once she'd got used to the water, she swam around making happy noises. When we climbed back out, the beach was empty and the sun had almost set.

I looked up and saw my classmates: eleven pairs of glimmering eyes directed straight at me. I walked towards the door, brushing the door handle as I went past. I then turned by the desk next to it, before continuing on back to my seat.

The rabbi sat with the side of his body against the desk, his back to the wall and the receiver nonchalantly pressed to his left ear. He seemed to devote more attention to the tangle of coiled lead that had formed between the receiver and the telephone than to the person with whom he was conversing. Without taking a pause from fingering the lead, he muttered a few terse opinions into the mouthpiece. 'That's impossible,' he said. 'Never.' And, 'Not in a million years.'

I was grateful that the telephone had interrupted us. Though I was starting to get used to the situation, I didn't like it. Even on Thursday afternoons, when the congregation building was practically empty, I was stopped for small chats on my way up to the third floor.

Sometimes, it was old friends of my parents who wanted to talk to me. Sometimes, it was people I'd seen in the synagogue for several years, but with whom I'd never previously exchanged a word. They first asked something normal, regarding school or the lessons about Israel, before starting on their real agenda: Mum's new husband; Dad's situation.

I saw every meeting as a test. My strategy to deal with them was never to look down at the floor, never to let my voice falter and never to let my eyes glaze over. To act like that was to admit defeat. Instead, I listened carefully while they were talking. I tried to look as though I was really paying attention to what they were saying, before adding some inappropriate gesture. A large smile, for instance. This confused them, and before they'd recovered their poise, I used to say that I had to rush off up to the classroom. It worked every time. After a few steps I used to turn around. They were always still standing there, in the exact same spot where I'd left them. When I saw them standing there, without a clue that they were being observed, it felt as though I had won.

The rabbi was different. He was more persistent than the others and his cramped office left no room to let your gaze waver for even a second. If the telephone hadn't rung, I wasn't sure which of us would have given up first.

'I'm sure you have some things you're wondering about,' the rabbi had said.

I had waited for a long time, as though I really needed to check my internal memos before I answered. I hadn't said anything about the only matter that really puzzled me. If everybody's reactions were understandable, I wondered, why were mine so questionable? If you were allowed to feel and think about anything, how could it be so dangerous not to think or feel anything in particular?

The window was open a few inches. The rabbi stood up and walked back and forth behind his chair. The phone cord got caught on the edge of the desk and he pulled the receiver hard. The large floor lamp started to sway. The phone dangled low over the desk, knocking over a brown plastic cup full of coffee. 'Fucking hell,' he hissed as the coffee poured over his desk, out over the piles of paper next to the typewriter, over the books which lay open and the notepads next to them.

He continued to swear, while he tucked the receiver in between his shoulder and ear, moving papers from the affected area. He also had to expend a great deal of effort convincing the person on the other end of the line that it wasn't him the expletives had been directed at. 'It was coffee... I just spilled coffee over my whole office,' he said, as he wiped the desk with a dirty T-shirt he'd found on the bookshelf.

He placed the coffee-stained papers one by one next to each other on the window ledge. When that was full, we put the papers on the dry parts of the floor.

'I don't know,' said the rabbi into the receiver, reaching reluctantly for the empty plastic cup.

'Instant coffee,' he said. 'From the machine.'

Then he said, 'Black.'

And then, 'Two, three. Never more than four.'

A long exposition followed from the other end of the line. The rabbi shouted back that he'd drunk his coffee black for twenty years without having any problems with his stomach. Then he said something in Hebrew before slamming down the phone.

'You'll be coming this Saturday, of course,' said Grandad, when I called him to tell him that Grandma had died.

I hadn't expected him to say anything else. He in turn couldn't reasonably have expected anything other than that I would sigh and answer, 'Maybe. We'll have to see.' But he still pretended to be surprised, as if it was the first time we'd spoken these lines to each other. 'Maybe? Now, you can't be serious, Jacob. Maybe?'

I didn't even try to defend myself. How could I explain to him why I didn't want to visit the synagogue without discussing the forbidden topics?

His voice was full of repressed rage. I really meant what I said; I hadn't ruled out going along, as I'd so often done before, but that wasn't enough for Grandad. 'Maybe' was bad enough, but once he'd begun to drink from the well of disappointment, he just couldn't stop.

'You'll have time to visit Mame at least?' he asked in a fierce tone, and I had to turn my mouth away so that he wouldn't hear me sighing again.

I leaned away from the phone until I'd gathered enough energy to deliver the next blow: 'Yes, maybe. I'll have to see what...'

The rest of the conversation just consisted of short phrases. I wanted to end the call so that I could bang my head against the wall. He wanted to end the call so that he could ring Aunt Irene and exchange indignant comments: not even when his own grandmother... and who will say *Kaddish* for me the day I... he'll regret it, believe me, he'll regret it for the rest of his life.

No matter what size slice of cake Grandad ate, it still seemed to be just at the limit of what his mouth could encompass. When he chewed, his cheeks turned into balls. His lips became a red and blue circle that spun pleasurably under his nose.

It was difficult for him to talk under such circumstances. In addition, his words were forced to compete with all the involuntary noises which emerged when he ate. There were smacking sounds of enjoyment from different parts of his body; all of his organs wanted to express their appreciation of what he filled them with.

Sometimes at their kitchen table, when I sat with Grandad next to me and Mame diagonally opposite, it was like finding oneself in an experimental sound workshop. Grunts from Grandad; clumsy slurpings from Mame. All of it seasoned with the Yiddish poisoned arrows that flew across the table at intervals of a few seconds. Oomph, oomph… slurp, slurp… *meshugenah*… oomph, oomph… slurp, slurp… *meshugenah.*

Mame had always seemed older than her years. In terms of physical and psychological ailments, of real and imaginary problems, she was worse affected than any of my other grandparents. Occasionally she called Dad late at night, coughed down the phone and said that he'd better come quickly, because it would soon all be over. She could feel death snapping at her heels, she told him. She said she was so close to the other side that she could reach out her hand and touch her mother's fingers. Even though these were obvious exaggerations, the silently accepted prognosis was that, of the four grandparents, she was the one who would pass away first. But, as though God had made a mistake, she still sat there, in front of the window, in her room on the second floor of the Jewish elderly care home, with her lower lip pouting, and her hand on the circular chest of drawers. She had outlived Grandma. Without doubt she was firmly determined to beat the remaining two as well.

The first time I noticed her increasing confusion was one afternoon, a week or so before the Christmas holidays, in my fifth year of secondary school. Mirra and I had taken the bus in. We sat next to each other at the kitchen table while Mame clattered with pots and pans. She told us that we'd each get a surprise once Grandad came home, when suddenly, in the midst of a sentence, she turned towards us with glazed eyes, before muttering a long, incomprehensible sentence. She stood like that for maybe one or two minutes. When she became her old self again it was as though she'd forgotten everything that had happened in the past few hours.

'Oh, but look, darling *kindlach*, are you here?'

She didn't want to move to the home. Shortly after that afternoon she stopped talking about Grandma, Grandpa and Mum when she called me in to dry the dishes. Instead she started whispering about Grandad and Aunt Irene. 'You have to help me,' she said. 'They want to get rid of me. I'll tell you what they've come up with now…' I told her that they weren't lying, that even Mirra and I had witnessed her attacks. It seemed as though she understood – 'Is that so?' she would say, with her washing-up-water-covered gherkin-sized finger pressed against her lower lip. 'Is that so?' – but only a few minutes later she'd forgotten and would return to her conspiracy theories.

Afterwards, Grandad would drive us home. He'd stop the car two blocks before he reached the house, rub his palm roughly against his grizzled cheek and say that things would work out with Mame. Eventually, he said, she'd agree to move.

The last time I'd been to the care home I'd made it to Mame's room and out again without bumping into anyone from the past. I'd acted as though I was absorbed by my mobile, walking out through the entrance, past the small car park, down the hill towards the city. I thought the danger was over, when I looked up and saw Bernie Friedkin's eyes through the windscreen of a black Mercedes SL 500.

The car continued on past me for a few yards before it stopped and the door opened. Bernie stepped out. The first thing that struck me was how dapper he looked. He wore a dark-beige coat which reached down a bit below his knees, had grey streaks on both temples and there was a large chain bracelet on his arm. In an inviting gesture, he indicated the inside of the car.

A little while later, Bernie pushed a glass of dark ale towards me, before telling me that it was the same sort that Jonathan and he used to drink. Jonathan lived in New York nowadays and every time Bernie was over they drank dark ale at their local, near to some wonderful square or other. Aha, I said and tried to sound as though I knew what he was talking about.

He had a lot to say about New York and Jonathan. That suited me fine. I could lean back and look at the Christmas shoppers who were stressing past in the rain outside, while amusing myself by silently imitating Bernie's boastfulness. When he went to the toilet, I took the opportunity to go through the pockets of the coat that he'd hung on the back of his chair. Apart from keys and a small diary which I unfortunately didn't have time to leaf through, I found a plain claret *kippah*. On the inside it read:

Susanna and Joram
Aug 16th
Palace Hotel
Jerusalem

The phrasing irritated me and at first I didn't understand why. Occasionally, I heard by word of mouth something about my old friends, that one of them had got engaged or been accepted by some university, but usually I didn't care. They had their lives and I had mine. I was convinced that I wouldn't have been able to stand more than ten seconds at any of their parties, so I shouldn't really bother myself now either.

It wasn't jealousy. It was something else that gnawed at me painfully when I learned that Sanna Grien had got married.

After we'd finished drinking, after Bernie had paid and I'd said no to the offer of a lift, and after he'd asked me to say hello to Mirra and Rafael, and then once again remarked upon the fact that it had been such a long time since we'd last met, we said our goodbyes in a manner indicating that it would be just as long before the next time. He walked to the car, while I walked in the opposite direction, past the shop windows, across the tramlines, through the city park, Brunnsparken, towards Drottningtorget Square, until I realized that what I saw around me wasn't the same town as the one I'd grown up in. There was no congregation building next to the canal; no synagogue with light-green domes. I found myself in another place now; a place I'd only heard about and where I thought I could never end up.

Västerås.

Ingemar had bought his favourite type of buttermilk. The packaging was white, with a sky-blue drawing in the middle. He showed Mirra and me how it should be served one Saturday afternoon when Mum wasn't at home. The buttermilk was thin and runny when you first poured it. You had to stir your spoon in it for a while before you could eat it. 'Slowly. Be careful,' said Ingemar when he thought Mirra was stirring too forcefully. He took hold of her wrist and guided it with even movements round and round the plate.

The buttermilk was sticky. Its taste was sharp, making you feel as if a thousand minute fireworks were exploding on your tongue. Ingemar told us that you should add lots of jam. Once we'd finished eating, both Mirra and I wanted another helping.

During the night I dreamed that Dad had walked towards me on a path in the woods. At first he smiled, but as he got closer his mouth grew narrow and he pronounced my name in a strained voice. 'It was you, Jacob,' he said. 'It was you who stuck the knife in.'

I sat up in bed. The water rushed through the pipes in the wall and I had to hold my hand in front of my mouth to avoid shouting out loud. I couldn't get back to sleep, so I opened the door carefully and sneaked down to the kitchen. There was a bowl next to the radio containing coins of different denominations. I was going to take the night bus. Surprise him. He'd make a bed up on the sofa for me. In the morning he'd give me a hundred-kronor note to buy us breakfast. 'Look,' the checkout girls would say when they saw me alone with my shopping trolley, 'so young and yet already mature enough to run a household.'

After breakfast, we'd each have a cup of coffee at the table. 'Thank you, Jacob,' he'd say. 'That was what I needed. Things will get better from now on, I promise you.'

I picked up four large coins. It made no difference to the bowl. I took another two. The stairs creaked. Ingemar's voice came from upstairs, muffled but still alert given the time: 'Hello?'

Heavy steps came down the stairs. I stood behind the open kitchen door, in the far corner. Feet padded across the brown kitchen floor. 'Hello? Jacob?' Over the threshold, towards the washing machine; a firm grip checked the outdoor handle.

I held my breath while the footsteps, now calmed, swept back to the kitchen. The lamp above the cooker flickered on. The rubber seal on the fridge door smacked as it was separated from the plastic edge inside. He lifted out something from the fridge, then poured milk into a glass. Crispbread crunched between his jaws. The clock ticked silently on the wall.

He refilled the glass once. When he'd wiped away the crumbs from the worktop, put the glass in the dishwasher and gone upstairs, I counted to 300 ticks of the clock. Then I went back up to bed.

After winning the second tournament of his career at the end of November, Amos Mansdorf climbed to eighteenth place in the ATP tennis rankings. It was Israel's highest position of all time. Two places higher than that which the nation's previous main contributor to world tennis – Shlomo Glickstein – had managed.

One advantage with Israeli sportsmen was that we could be certain that they were Jews. With athletes of other nationalities there was doubt involved. Names could sound Jewish without being so. Appearances could be deceptive. Everything was riddled with uncertainty. In his moments of doubt, Dad wouldn't even commit with 100 per cent certainty as to where the American baseline specialist Aaron Krickstein had his religious home.

The news about Mansdorf was one of the few positive items that reached us from Israel during those weeks. The autumn's heated atmosphere culminated one December afternoon when an Israeli lorry driver lost control of his vehicle, before colliding with another lorry full of Palestinian workers. Four of them died. Incited by the rumour that the collision wasn't an accident, an uprising began that evening in the Jabalia refugee camp, which quickly spread across Gaza and the West Bank. During the days which followed, TVs around the world were filled with images of nine-year-olds throwing stones against one of the world's most powerful armies. Blurry pictures showed three soldiers beating up a protester.

In Gothenburg, the temperature dropped. The water in the canal froze and the first snow of winter fell outside the synagogue's windows. Hanukkah arrived and extra security

115

personnel had to be called in to protect the congregation building. During the first evening of the festival, about a hundred members gathered to see the rabbi light a flare and climb up a ladder, before lighting the first candle on the large wooden *menorah* that had been assembled in the courtyard.

The following morning, the rabbi knocked on the door to Zaddinsky's office. He sat in the armchair, rested his elbows on his thighs and explained that he'd been offered a job in his homeland that he was going to accept.

I had been given a light-brown leather jacket by Mum and Ingemar as a Hanukkah present. It had elbow patches sewn on it and I spent a large portion of the first days of the Christmas holidays wearing it in front of the bathroom mirror.

One afternoon, Dad and I went to the cinema and saw a Mel Brooks film. Dad had started working again, for just a few days to begin with. After the film, when we sat in the café opposite the cinema, he said that he might join some work colleagues on a skiing trip to Norway between Christmas and New Year. I said that was a great idea.

He gave me a lift home, then beeped his horn at me as he drove off again. After dinner, I put on my jacket and said that I was going out to see a friend. It was cold, but the wind wasn't blowing. I walked slowly around the neighbourhood with my hands in my jacket pockets. Past the football pitch, the sandpits and the hill where we sledged when it snowed. On the noticeboard on a floor of the multi-storey car park there was a note about children's lost rubber boots, along with a summary of a small festival that had been held in October. Only one of the street lamps was working on the hill through the woods and I half-ran through the darkest parts. Two girls were sitting on swings in the playground outside the daycare centre. One of them had a thin pink lighter which she kept clicking with her thumb. She wanted to try on my jacket, letting me in turn try on hers: a large red winter jacket with curly fur lining its hood.

For the most part, I stayed in my room and drew on my writing pad. Sometimes Mirra came in with the *Göteborgs Posten* newspaper and pointed at various TV programmes she wanted us to watch. One day, I asked her to help me move my bed from one end of the room to the other. We pushed in the desk below the diagonally sloping roof, then covered the wall underneath the window with pages we'd cut out of old comics.

The living room was full of chocolate boxes which Ingemar had received as Christmas presents from different companies and authorities. He placed the largest one on the table. As soon as it was emptied, another one replaced it. On Christmas Eve, Mum roasted a turkey, which she served with red cabbage and Brussels sprouts, along with cranberry jelly in small glasses. Grandma said she'd never eaten anything as delicious in her entire life. Mirra asked Ingemar if he was disappointed that he wasn't able to eat his usual Christmas dinner, but he assured her that he wasn't.

On Christmas Day, his daughter came by, together with her boyfriend. Shortly before they arrived, Mum and Ingemar had some sort of disagreement in the kitchen. Ingemar's hands were still shaking when he poured the wine during dinner.

When I went to bed that evening, I noticed that my throat was sore and that it hurt when I swallowed. In the morning the symptoms had developed into a stubborn, rattling cough. I talked to Dad on the phone. He told me to cough into the mouthpiece, before spelling out the name of a medicine I was to ask Mum to buy. He was going to Norway the following afternoon. He told me that Bernie had got him a new skiing jacket and trousers. He would rent skis and boots when he was there. There were five of them going on the trip, sharing two rooms in an apartment hotel a short distance from the piste. He would be away for three days. He also said that he wanted us to meet up as soon as he got back.

What he didn't say was that, a few hours after he'd put the phone down, he'd buy a takeaway from the Chinese restaurant across the street. Or that, after he'd finished eating, he'd put the half-full cartons in a white plastic bag, tie the handles in a tight knot and place the bag outside his front door. Neither did he say that, after an additional few hours, he would pull out an envelope containing A4 writing paper from a folder in the bookcase and put it on the kitchen table. Nor that he would then sit there and drink a glass of water, which he would swallow together with the contents of a small brown and yellow bottle which normally stood high up on a shelf in his bathroom cabinet. He didn't say that he would then stand up so quickly that the chair behind him fell over. Or that he himself would then fall over, before hitting the kitchen worktop, and end up with two small bruises just above his left eyebrow.

I didn't find that out until the following morning.

After breakfast, Mirra remained seated at the table and read with her palm pressed against her cheek. I cleared Ingemar's and her plates from the table, along with mine, then washed away the crumbs that had got stuck to the porcelain. Ingemar looked up gratefully at me from his newspaper, before offering to clear away the remainder of the items on the table. At some point during the morning, he'd found out that I'd never been to an ice hockey match and he'd promised that we would go and see one before the end of the Christmas holidays. Mum had put her coffee cup on top of the washing machine. When we'd emptied the tumble dryer, she turned her back to it, took a large gulp and lit a cigarette. My throat had got better, but she still had errands to do in town, so we might as well stop by at the chemist's, she said.

She gave me a warm and sweet-smelling pile of towels and sheets to carry upstairs. In the large bedroom I got caught up reading a copy of *National Geographic* which lay open on Ingemar's bedside table. I then collected the note from my room on which I'd written the name of the cough medicine. I was walking downstairs again when the phone rang. It rang out twice before Mirra answered. She handed over the phone to Mum, looking puzzled when we met in the hall at the bottom of the stairs. She was still wearing her nightie. It was patterned with yellow and pink stripes, but was a bit too long at the arms. Sometimes she would lift her sleeves up to her mouth and chew them. I sat down in the armchair in front of the mirror. I folded the note in my hand into a tiny, compact square, before unfolding it again. Mirra looked at my hand and asked me what I was doing. The next thing I remember is Mum staggering out of the kitchen and collapsing on the dining-room table.

For the rest of the day, the living room slowly filled up with people. Some just stayed for a short time; others remained all day until the evening. Bernie didn't take off his jacket when he arrived. He leaned back against the dining-room table and exchanged a few brief words with Mum, without either of them looking each other in the eyes. After a while, he approached Mirra and me, hunching down in front of us. He said that he was going to the hospital and asked if we wanted to join him. I looked first at Mirra, then at him. I tried to imagine what it would be like there: a nurse, a bed, a table on wheels, long beige curtains. I shook my head, but regretted it almost immediately after he'd driven off.

During the week that followed, people continued to drop by. Old uncles rang the doorbell and handed over bags of groceries from the kosher food shop. Old aunties handed over trays of pastries, together with a long list of instructions: warm it at such and such a temperature, don't forget to add a dollop of cream and for God's sake don't freeze it. Some of them came in, sat for a while in the kitchen and talked about how small I'd been the last time they'd seen me.

In the afternoons, Papa Moysowich conducted the religious service in the living room. He had collected a small ark for the Torah scroll, along with a set of chairs from the congregation. Mirra and I helped to carry them in, placing them in front of the window in two rows: one to the left for the men and one to the right for the women. Outside it was pitch dark. The garden was a grey and white mixture of snow and water. There were only enough chairs for the old people, so I stood up during the service. When it got boring, I started making faces at Mirra. One afternoon, towards the end of a service, I started to laugh while I was pulling a face at her. Mum looked angrily at me and I heard small sighs spread quickly across the room. I held both hands across my mouth and tried to think about something dull, but it didn't help. I just laughed more and more, until finally I had to go up to my room and calm down.

In Mame and Grandad's flat the mirrors had been covered with sheets. All the photos of Dad had been removed. I didn't know if this was some old religious tradition or if they just didn't want to see his face for a while.

The day after the funeral, Mame lay in bed. Mirra and I sat next to each other on two chairs by the side of the bed. Mame's lower lip was shaking. Her words came forth in bursts. When I stood up to go to the toilet, her cold white hand emerged from under the sheet and squeezed my wrist hard. Grandad sat in his armchair with his arms folded. His chest moved slowly up and down. One hand drummed angrily against his upper arm. Mirra asked some questions and he answered curtly, without lifting his head to look at her.

The following four Saturday mornings I met him in the synagogue to say *Kaddish*. Grandad read from his light-brown *siddur*. It was so small that he could hold it in one hand. He had brought it with him on his escape to Sweden as a refugee, hidden in some extra compartment somewhere, and it had survived without a mark. During the weeks he stored it in a hard plastic box in the upper desk drawer in the study.

On our fourth and last Saturday, there weren't more than about ten or so people in the synagogue apart from us. No women, just men who stood far apart from one another, spread out across the pews. The sun didn't rise until quite a while into the service and was anyway too weak to push in through the patterned windows. We had gone up to the ark and walked back to our seats when Grandad silently lowered his face to the book-rest. The small prayer book fell from his hands, straight down on to the worn floorboards. I picked it up, then did what you were supposed to do: kissed it on the Star of David embossed on the front cover. For several days afterwards, I was aware of the dusty taste on my lips.

When we parted that Saturday, Grandad handed over a plastic folder containing four letters. One each for Mum, myself and my siblings, written on smooth paper with a medical logo in the top right-hand corner.

I sat on the floor in my room and read it. Dad's handwriting was rapid and expansive, with large loops around the lettering. Furthest up was my name, my complete Hebrew one, which also contained his name and Grandad's. I heard Dad's voice as I read, almost as clearly as if he'd been kneeling next to my bed and stroking his hand against my forehead.

On one of the last occasions we'd met, we'd eaten kebabs. Strong red sauce dripped through the bread and paper, down on to the table. We sat next to each other on bar stools in the kebab-shop window.

Dad smiled when he felt my leg jump up and rest on his thighs. It was nothing I could control; my leg just ended up there of its own accord part of the way through every meal. He swung his leg a little, then we both laughed when he, between mouthfuls, imitated an unpleasant patient he'd had the day before. I thought about the fact that his laughter didn't immediately die away, that traces remained in his face for a long time afterwards. I also thought that the skin under his eyes wasn't as grey any more and that his hair once again looked full-bodied.

Even his voice, which throughout the whole autumn had been weak and uncertain, had its usual energy when he talked about the methods his colleagues used to foist a difficult patient on someone else.

I saw their staff room in front of me as he talked. It smelled of coffee and cigarette smoke. There was a vending machine further down the corridor, where Dad used to buy me a small box of tiny square salt sweets. A green coin-operated telephone was on the wall next to the machine. I imagined that it was from this phone that Dad's colleague had called.

Almost four months had gone by since that phone call. I still thought about it often before I went to sleep, trying to imagine what had happened. He had taken the car to work that morning as my father. Three days later he came back as someone I didn't know, someone who didn't know me. Since then, Dad's old familiar personality had only been glimpsed on occasion. I hadn't dared to ask him what had happened. I didn't want to remind him of something that might make him feel even worse.

Dad sucked on a green chilli pepper with an expression of fear and delight. When I finally asked him the question, he took the chilli pepper from his mouth and put it with the remains of the onions and the mixture of sauce and fat that had collected in the thin kebab paper. He said that he'd been about to do something very foolish. I wasn't entirely sure what he meant, but I didn't ask any more questions.

He put his wallet on the table in front of us. When I'd finished eating, I looked through it. The billfold was full of receipts. He had a Visa card, plus an American Express gold card that I knew he was proud of. A tiny version of an old studio photograph was there, flattened between the card slots. Mum was laughing, holding Mirra on her knee. Rafael had tinted pilot's sunglasses. Next to him sat Dad, while I stood at the front with a broad smile and wide eyes.

Shortly after I handed back the wallet, I saw a teacher from school pass by on the pavement outside the window. I crouched down quickly, then lifted up my jacket collar in order to shield my face.

We walked to the car park in silence. The car was icy cold, but Dad didn't start the engine. Matches lay abandoned on the rubber mat in front of my shoes. A throat lozenge had got covered in hair and was stuck on the edge, up towards the gear stick.

'… to lie, Jacob, to be sloppy…'

Dad held his hands together. The keys in the ignition rattled every time he accidentally knocked them.

'… to hide, to sweep things under the carpet…'

The clouds lowered themselves over the cranes in the harbour. The sky, the ground and the sea had all melted together into one single light-grey surface. Dad leaned forward, lifted my hands from my ears, then forced me to lift up my head.

'… the same mistake. This is serious, Jacob. Do you understand what I'm saying?'

He repeated his warnings in the letter. Despite the circumstances, it was otherwise a mostly positive letter. He lavished compliments and praise on me, and I imagined that he had smiled a little to himself as he wrote it. The only thing that referred to his situation, along with what he was about to do, was a sentence down at the bottom of the page.

A long handwritten line had been crossed out several times. Right next to it, in small letters, almost out at the margin, it said, 'You'll be better off without me.'

I took the letter with me when I moved out. By that time, I hadn't read it for several years. It had remained in its plastic folder, and every time I'd seen it, I'd thought that I'd take it out at the right time. Mirra, Mum and Ingemar waved goodbye to me at the station. After three hours of travelling, I had to change trains. I bought a packet of cigarettes at the kiosk, then sat down on a bench in the sun. I emptied my pockets, and the outer compartment of my bag, which was sealed with a zip. I made sure that I had all my important documents with me: my train tickets; the letter of acceptance to the university; my phone card; and the note with the number of the person whose student room I'd be renting.

When the train arrived, everything was lying in my lap. I hastily gathered it all up, then hurried across the platform. At the last moment, an old grey-haired lady caught up with me, waving my wallet, which I'd forgotten. As I took it, I saw Dad's letter lying on the ground, underneath the bench, but I didn't run back to get it.

The room I'd rented contained a desk, an armchair, a bed and a bookshelf with literature from courses my landlord had attended. A red and yellow piece of cloth hung on the wall. During the first few terms, I went home for the big religious festivals, but after a while I started saying to Mum and Grandad that I would be celebrating with a Jewish couple I'd met at the university. On those occasions I did go to Gothenburg, I more and more frequently didn't tell Mum or Grandad at all. I stayed with a friend, avoiding those parts of the city and the streets they might visit.

Rafael and Papa Moysowich were sitting at the dinner table and reading something from the *siddur*. Mirra had gone upstairs with Grandpa. Before Aunt Betty's taxi arrived, she'd walked once around the table and placed the remaining pastries and biscuits in a napkin, which she'd then carefully folded up and put in her handbag.

Grandad had sunk down on the sofa and looked straight ahead through half-closed eyes. He hadn't moved from his seat since he'd sat down. Every time I'd been away – gone to the toilet or carried something into the kitchen – he'd called me back to the space at his side on the sofa. I liked that. Despite the circumstances, I still felt calm from sitting close to him, feeling the warmth from his body. I looked at his ape-like paws, which lay on top of each other across the buttons of his shirt, and felt the urge to say something kind and appreciative. I emptied my glass and was just about to put a hand on his shoulder when he stood up. He pushed himself forward between the table and the sofa. Ingemar was quickly by his side to support him and help him to the bathroom upstairs. When Grandad came down again, he said it was time to go home.

He wasn't in a hurry to put on his outdoor coat. When he'd buttoned his coat up, he thanked Ingemar for his hospitality with a firm handshake. He cuddled my siblings, craned his neck to one side and waved to the people who were still in the living room. There then followed a few unbearable seconds before Mum and he made up their minds about how to say goodbye.

I had offered to follow him home and stood with my jacket on by the door. My clothes were itching. I didn't dare look up from the floor during the moments when Grandad and Mum were uncertain as to how to say farewell. I dared even less when they finally decided to embrace each other.

The last thing that happened before we left was that Grandad put his hand in his coat pocket and unfolded a document. The outside door was open. Grandad stood just inside the threshold and repeated the contents of the document from memory, while he let the official paper itself get passed around. The burial society needed to know that we'd been informed of its new rules, that we realized the practical circumstances which had brought about the rule change, as well as what importance their observance had for future Jewish life in Gothenburg.

Mum looked at the piece of paper and confirmed her awareness of the new rules with her signature.

The pale late-winter sun had practically set. A lonely tram rattled down the street. Grandad's walking stick scratched against the damp grit on the pavement. We said goodbye to Aunt Irene, then continued on round the corner, past the tobacconist's, up the hill and in through the cold doorway to his apartment building. On the outer front door were the remains of a sticker I'd put there a long time ago. The weak outline of a glue stain on the brown metal served as a reminder of the parts that had been scraped away. The banister was a long white tube that spiralled up to the first floor. Grandad was breathing with his mouth open when he put the key in the lock.

The warmth of the flat was in stark contrast to the outer corridor. The lamp in the hall flickered on, then spread a gentle light across the patterned carpet, Mame's paintings and the small decorative menagerie she'd placed on the metal shelf along the wall. Grandad put his gloves down on the chest of drawers in front of the mirror. He took off his shoes with a shoehorn, hung his coat on a hanger, then put his walking stick in a wooden container next to the shoe stand. Having washed his hands and face, he walked into the bedroom.

Yesterday's *Göteborgs Tidningen* newspaper was folded up on the bench underneath the lopsided cupboard in the kitchen. The sink and the draining stand were both empty, and I guessed that Aunt Irene had been there recently and tidied away everything. The fridge was full of cheese and pickled vegetables, as well as plastic boxes with red lids and beige tape stuck on them labelling their contents.

I filled a glass with water, then took it to Grandad's bed.

The light from the hall shone into the room. Grandad used

his elbows to raise his upper body. The glass of water shook and spilled a few drops when he put it back down.

The bedstead knocked against the wall when Grandad moved.

'Grandad,' I said, then pushed my index finger between his shoulders.

He turned his head over his shoulder.

'When Dad was small,' I continued, while waiting for his forehead to compress in concentration, 'did he lie on your shins and then talk to you?'

I lay on the floor in order to demonstrate what I meant. Grandad shifted over on to his side. His palm rubbed his chin in rough, large movements. His eyes shifted between me and the ceiling, and I could see the gap in his upper jaw where a molar had been. He asked me to repeat my demonstration. Then his arm came down and squeezed my cheek.

'No,' he said. 'I can't remember him doing that.'

He turned back again and soon his breathing got heavier. I adjusted the sheet over him, then dried the bedside table with my sleeve. I walked into the living room and played a few chords on the piano, before looking for old photos and letters in the dark-brown chest of drawers next to the window. I couldn't find anything of interest there and I was on my way out into the hall when I stopped in front of the bookshelf. I bent down to the bottom shelf. The plastic cover was stiff, but the arm responded surprisingly quickly once I'd freed it from the tag that was holding it in place. The inner sleeve rustled when I pulled the record out of its colourful jacket. Through the transparent plastic, a green label was visible, along with the words 'Melody Grand Prix' in bold, black letters.

The turntable had already begun to spin. Holding my palms against the thin edge, I guided the hole over the peg.

Epilogue

Grandad died in his bathtub one summer day three years later. After the funeral everyone went back to the care home. Mame had been wheeled down from the second floor and sat at the far end of the table. Nothing in her expression suggested that she understood why we had gathered there. I sat my eight-month-old daughter in her lap. Mame shoved pastries in between her lips, but shook her head in annoyance when I said she was the girl's great-grandmother.

Afterwards we took the lift upstairs with Mame. An Israeli woman of about forty-five pushed her down the corridor. Once inside the room, she lifted Mame over to the armchair, then gave her three pills, which she was to wash down with a clear red liquid.

Mame fell asleep for a few minutes. When she woke up, she apologized for not having anything to offer us to eat. She looked carefully around the room, as if there might be a slim chance that the simple furnishings concealed a coffee percolator or a biscuit tin somewhere.

Her eyes fixed on the circular chest of drawers. She raised a finger and told me to pull out the top drawer.

'Go ahead now. Pull it open,' she said, when she noticed that I was hesitating.

Three green and grey folders were lying next to each another. Thin rubber bands had been wrapped round the middle of them. On all the covers, a company name was printed in old-fashioned lettering above a box with thin lines.

The only thing that distinguished the covers from one another were the names Grandad had written down in the bottom right-hand corner.

When I lifted up the one which had 'Jacob' written on it, a piece of paper fell out. Mame reached for the folder, before pointing at a spot on the floor next to the armchair, where she thought I should stand.

It took her a long time to remove the rubber band. Inside the covers there was a large sheaf of papers in various sizes, made of differing materials. A wish list I'd made for Hanukkah, along with a list I'd made in the third year of junior school of the ten songs that I liked the most at that time. There was an English test from the first year of secondary school and a large number of drawings. Mame took out one at a time, handed them over to me, then watched me at a side angle from below, with an expectant look on her face.

'It's my grandson who's done them,' she said.

She explained the background to every drawing. One of them she'd received on her birthday. Another featured a motif that her husband had asked her grandson to draw. She reported factually and accurately about her grandson's examination results, the university courses I'd taken and girlfriends I'd had. She told me to pick up the piece of paper that had fallen to the floor. When I handed it over, I saw that it was the drawing of King Louie that had been on their bedroom wall. The orangutan was holding a banana in one hand and looking in surprise over his shoulder. Mame gazed at it for a long time.

'We're very proud of him,' she said, and asked me to put the folder back in the drawer.

Glossary

bar mitzvah	the religious initiation ceremony for a Jewish boy when he reaches the age of thirteen
baruch hashem	expression: 'Thank God'
bat mitzvah	the religious initiation ceremony for a Jewish girl when she reaches the age of thirteen
bima	raised platform in front of the ark in synagogue
brucha	a blessing or prayer
chevra	group of friends; also used as abbreviation for Chevra Kadisha, the burial society
drek	excrement; rubbish
farkakte	shitty
fershteyn	understand
feygele	little bird; slang for male homosexual
forts	fart
goy	Gentile
hanukkiah	nine-branched candelabrum used during festival of Hanukkah
'Hatikvah'	Israeli national anthem
kacker	crap; very small thing
Kaddish	prayer for the dead
kashrut	dietary laws
kibbutz (pl. *kibbutzim*)	Israeli communal farming settlement
kiddush	blessing recited over wine, performed at meal after religious service
kindlach	children
kippah (pl. *kippot*)	skullcap

kosher	fit to eat according to dietary laws
l'chaim	to life (used as a toast)
mazel tov	congratulations: 'Good luck'
menorah	seven-branched candelabrum
meshugenah	mad
mezuzah (pl. *mezuzot*)	small oblong container holding religious scroll, fixed to doorpost
mishegas	madness
mohel	ritual circumciser
nebbishdikke	weak
nu	interrogative expression: 'So?'
putz	stupid person
scheiss	shit
schtunken	stink
schweig	silence
Seder	the ceremony and meal that take place at the festival of Pesach
Shabbat	Sabbath
shikse	Gentile woman
shkoyach	congratulations: 'Good on you'
shul	synagogue
siddur	prayer book
tallit	prayer shawl
tefillin	phylacteries
tzorres	troubles

About the translator

Michael Lundin was born in Stockholm in 1967, and was educated in England, Scotland and Sweden. This is his first translation of a novel. He lives in Brighton.